GOOD BOY

BOOK ONE OF THE GOOD BOY, BAD BOY DUET

MEGAN LOWE

Cover Design: Pretty In Ink Creations

Editing: Hot Tree Editing

Formatting: Pretty In Ink Creations

Paperback: 978-0-6486536-1-5

❀ Created with Vellum

For the ones who always see the good in people;
For the ones who always want to help;
For the ones who fall in love with the bad boy, even when they
know better.

For Jason Dupasquier.
Ride in Peace Ja50n.

CONNOR

Connor (18):

New to town and looking for someone to get to know, maybe show me the sights.

Likes: cars, all things Detroit, and hopefully you.

Dislikes: slow cars, bullshit, Mitch Trubisky.

CHAPTER 1

It's a fact universally acknowledged that teenage boys are horny fucks. It's *also* a fact that when you take away a teenage boy's regular piece of ass, they're going to want a new one. And soon. I've heard a build-up of semen fucks with your brain. I've also heard it can drive you crazy. And since I *really* don't want that to happen to me, I go back to swiping.

Too fat. Too old. Too geeky. Too hairy.

I throw my phone down.

"There are zero datable men in this city," I lament to my younger brother, Jase.

"It's Chicago," he answers, not even bothering to look up.

"Exactly! That means there should be a ton more eligible men here than in Triple Falls." Triple Falls, our former hometown. The hometown we left two weeks ago.

"Please tell me you two have done more than sit on the couch all day?" Amy, our older sister, says as she breezes in.

"Yup," I reply. "We got up, made food, showered—you know, essential stuff."

She sighs as she dumps her purse on the kitchen counter. "I suppose I should be grateful you're at least doing that."

"Mmm," I agree, picking up my phone again and continuing to swipe left.

She huffs and moves around the kitchen, doing whatever it is she's doing.

I love my sister, I do, but I'm a seventeen-year-old guy —I don't like anyone on principal. But when my twenty-three-year-old sister suddenly became guardian to me and our fifteen-year-old brother? It was never going to end well. And it's not like it's Amy's fault. It's not anyone's fault, unless you want to blame God or whoever invented cancer. To watch one parent be ravaged by that fucking disease is gut-wrenching. To watch *both*? It does things to a guy. And then, mercifully, when their suffering is over, you find your older sister is handed guardianship and your life is uprooted and transplanted here, to Chicago, a few weeks short of starting your senior year. Fun times.

"Dinner's ready, you guys," she calls.

Jase jumps up with the enthusiasm only a fifteen-year-old going through a growth spurt can muster.

I follow at a more sedate pace, earning myself a glare when I finally sit down.

"What?" I say as I help myself to kung pao chicken and rice.

"You start school soon," Amy says.

"I know."

"It's your senior year."

"I know."

"How are you feeling about it?"

I shrug. "It's school."

"It's important. If you do well, that could mean a scholarship."

"Aims...."

"Con...."

I sigh.

"I know this isn't how you pictured your senior year—"

I snort.

"—and you know I'd give anything for things to go back to how they were—"

"How they were?" I ask. "How they were was me at *fourteen* trying to hold the house together because Mom was too busy looking after Dad to worry about me, about Jase. It was watching him slowly waste away and knowing there was nothing I could do. It was trying to reassure Jase everything would be all right when I knew that was the furthest thing from the truth. It was feeling relieved, so fucking *relieved* when he finally died because it meant he wasn't in pain anymore. And then, if that weren't enough, it was being fucking gutted when Mom's diagnosis came through. And where were you, huh? Here, going to your fancy school, living your fabulous life while we had to watch them die." I shove away from the table. "But I guess everything's fine now because you're here and you know this isn't how I saw my senior year playing out."

I stomp to my room and slam the door. I know I should feel grateful Amy took us in. She didn't have to, but all I can think of is how she wasn't there when it mattered. That I had to shoulder everything Mom and Dad went through because she couldn't leave her life here.

I flop onto my bed, ignoring the creaking it makes. I pull out my phone, logging into Poundr again.

Too fat. Too old. Too hairy. Too pretty. The next image on the screen stops me in my tracks. Usually the profile pics are selfies, maybe even a group shot or photos taken in front of a generic landmark. This one is just this guy's hand. That's it. One hand. Five fingers and a tiny star-shaped scar in between his thumb and index finger. Ordinarily I would say there's nothing special about a hand, but…. There's something about *this* one. Throwing caution to the wind, I swipe right and am pleasantly surprised when the match is confirmed. Almost immediately, a message pops up from "James."

James: Hey.

That's it. One word. Three little letters.

So I reply how any sane seventeen-year-old guy replies.

Connor: Hey.

Now, it's *totally* my imagination—because how could it be anything other than that? I don't know this guy from Adam—but I *swear* I can feel a wry chuckle coming from the other end of our chat.

James: What's up?

Now, if I were a different type of guy, I'd reply "me," but I was raised with manners, so I go with:

Connor: Not much. Hiding from my family, no big

deal.

James: Literally or figuratively?

Well, isn't "James" pulling out the big words?

Connor: Literally. My sister.... My life's just a mess right now.

I don't know why I'm telling a complete stranger this, but just as I don't know why I swiped right on just a hand, there's something... compelling about him.

James: Join the club.

Connor: Families blow.

James: Agreed.

Connor: So tell me, James, what sort of stuff are you into?

James: Besides matching with cute guys who apparently have similarly screwed up family lives?

My heart does a flip when he says I'm cute.

Connor: Yeah, besides that.

James: The usual. Baseball, blowjobs, and Bentleys.

Connor: Ah, the three B's, essential for life. Sox or Cubs?

James: Please, Cubs.

Connor: I thought most Chicagoans were Sox people?

James: Only losers root for the Sox. You're new to town, right?

Connor: Just moved here last week from Michigan.

James: You liking it?

Connor: The city's fine, it's just....

James: Your sister.

He catches on quick. I like that.

Connor: Yeah. Plus, I'm about to start my senior year and a move, it's not ideal.

James: High school senior?

Connor: Yeah. Is that a problem?

I quickly flick to his profile and see he's eighteen. Technically, my profile says I am too, but only because that's how old you have to be in order to use the app. I'll be eighteen in a month.

James: Nope. I might be one myself.

Connor: Nice. Have you heard of Windswept Academy? That's where I'm starting.

James: I know a few guys who go there.

Connor: What's it like? Do you know?

According to Amy, Windswept is one of Chicago's best schools, and Jase and my attendance was mandated in our parents' wills should Amy move us to Chicago.

James: It's fine. I hear there's a major prick there who practically runs the school.

Connor: Sounds like trouble.

James: I think it's fine if you stay out of his way.

Connor: Thanks for the tip.

Staying out of this guy's way won't be a problem. Causing problems and bringing attention to myself is the last thing I want to do. All I want to do is get this year over and done with.

James: No problems. A guy on the baseball team died last summer. Rumor has it Cav was involved.

Connor: Holy shit.

James: Yeah.

Connor: Did the police investigate him?

James: His mom's one of the senators for Illinois, and his dad owns like, half of the city.

Connor: So that's a no. Aren't people afraid of him?

James: I think he likes it, you know, he gets off on it. The fear, the power.

Connor: That's fucked up.

James: That's Cavanaugh McLaughlin for you.

CHAPTER 2

Over the next week, James becomes a bit of a lifesaver, an escape, a reprieve. I know Amy is doing the best she can, but all I can think is it's too little, too late.

"Would you put that phone down, *please*, Connor?" she asks as we attempt a "family" meal. "Who *are* you talking to, anyway? That thing is practically glued to your palm."

"Do you actually care or are you asking because it's something you think you *should* ask?"

She puts down her knife and fork. "I'm trying here, Con."

"*Now*," I correct. "You're trying *now*."

"That's not fair."

"Don't talk to me about fair," I grit out. "Fair would've been you coming to help us out when Dad got sick. Or when he died. Or when Mom got sick, but no, you had to stay here. Stuff whatever me and Jase were going through."

She lowers her head. I know I'm being a dick, but I don't care. I've got years of anger pent up, and it's coming out.

"We needed you, Aims, and you never came. Then, when you finally did, you were barely there long enough to say 'hi' before you packed us up and moved us here."

"You couldn't stay in Michigan by yourselves," she says.

"Did you ever even consider moving there?" I ask.

She ducks her head again.

"We were at a good school. We had friends, people who knew what we've gone through, who understood us, who wanted to be there for us. What do we have here?"

"You have me, each other."

"Do we *really* have you?"

"Of course you do."

"Because your past actions say otherwise."

"I'm trying," she says in a small voice.

"Try harder," I hit back as I push away from the table and disappear into my room.

Connor: You there?

His response comes almost immediately.

James: What's up?

Connor: Why do families suck so much?

I can almost hear his wry chuckle again.

James: You're asking the wrong person.

Connor: Want to vent?

James: Yes and no.

I chuckle.

Connor: Yeah, me too.

For a while, there's nothing but silence before I pick up my phone again.

Connor: It's my sister. She was nowhere when our parents got sick, then when they died she swept in and moved our little brother and me here. What's with that?

James: I will see your shitty sister and raise you an overbearing mother and a largely useless father.

Connor: Dysfunctional families, keeping therapists in business since forever.

James: Lol.

I startle when there's a knock at my door.

"Yeah?" I call.

Jase pops his head in. "You okay?" he asks.

I blow out a breath as he comes in and sits on the edge of my bed. "What do you think?"

He shrugs.

"Am I being too harsh?" I ask.

"Yes, and no."

I chuckle. "That's helpful."

"I mean, yeah, it sucks Aims wasn't there through all the shit stuff with Mom and Dad, and yeah, it sucks she moved us here, but I don't think this is going to suck too bad."

"*Too bad*," I repeat. "That's… optimistic."

He shrugs again.

"I do think you need to cut her some slack though. What happened wasn't her fault, Con."

"Aren't you angry?" I ask.

"Sure, but I also know holding on to that anger won't

get me anything. It won't bring them back, it won't change Amy's response, it won't move us back to Michigan."

"She just left us, Jase."

"Maybe she had her reasons."

"What reason could excuse her abandoning her younger brothers?"

"Maybe you should ask her that."

"And maybe you should stop being so fucking smart," I say, pushing him with my foot.

"I know watching Mom and Dad…. It sucked, majorly, and I know you took on a lot of my stuff—"

"I did that willingly," I interject. "That was never a burden. *You* were never a burden, Jase. You were just a kid. Hell, you're *still* a kid."

"And so are you."

"I'll be eighteen in a month."

"*In a month.* Meaning you're seventeen now, which is less than eighteen, the age at which you legally become an adult, making you still a kid."

"Anyone ever tell you you're too clever for your own good?"

"I take after my brother."

I sit up and ruffle his hair. "You're all right sometimes, you know that?"

"Yeah, I do."

We both laugh.

"Just give Aims a chance, Con. She's doing the best she can. We all are."

I run a hand through my sandy-blond hair.

"Just give her a chance. That's all I'm asking."

I open my mouth, but he continues.

"For me? Please?"

"I make no promises," I warn.

"I'm just asking you to try."

I nod. "Okay."

Jase tackle hugs me. "Thank you, Con. You're the best."

I ruffle his hair again. "Only for you, you know that, right?"

"Look, I know you like to think you're a badass and all that, but I hate to break it to you, you're really not."

"Pfft, I *so* am."

He rolls his eyes. "Whatever you say."

He gets up and heads to the door. He turns before he walks through. "She is trying, Con. I know it may seem too little, too late, but at least she's here now. Things could've been a lot worse for us."

I nod. "I know." And I do; it's just after everything that's happened over the past few years, what she's doing? It doesn't feel enough. I'm a little scared it will never feel enough either.

Amy and I used to be close. Then things changed. *She* changed. A distance opened up between us, and as time wore on, that gap only got bigger. When she graduated, she moved here for school, and that was all she wrote. Now, here I am.

I know I'm putting Jase in the middle of whatever's between us. I know it's a really shitty thing to do—he's innocent in all this—but the resentment I feel against her…. It's all consuming.

My phone chirps on my side table.

James: You know if you, I dunno, want to talk about it, or not, I'm here.

My thing with Amy might take up a lot of energy, but maybe I *might* find some room for James; you know, purely to blow off steam.

CHAPTER 3

J ames: **Tell me the weirdest place you've gotten some.**

I chuckle. It's safe to say in the past week James and I have gotten... closer, more familiar with each other.

Things with Amy are... well, they're not worse and they're not better, so I guess that means they're the same. I know I told Jase I'd try, but I don't know if I really feel like I can, or even know how to at this point.

But James.... He's distraction enough.

Connor: It'd be a toss-up between a blowjob in a janitor's closet in Michigan General, or a hand job in geography class. You?

James: Geography class?

Connor: What can I say? Borders make me horny.

James: I'll keep that in mind.

Connor: You do that, but you still haven't answered your half of the question.

James: Either backstage at a press conference or under the stage at a fundraising dinner.

Connor: Exhibitionist?

He sends back winking face emojis.

James: Never knock back an opportunity, right?

Connor: Right

Connor: How old were you when you lost your virginity?

James: Sixteen.

Connor: So not-so-sweet sixteen?

He sends back some eye rolling emojis.

James: You?

Connor: Fifteen. Johnny Black. My mom asked him to check on my brother and me while my dad was in the hospital. God, that guy was built.

James: Lol. Your dad was sick?

Connor: Cancer. He died a couple of years ago. My mom passed just a month ago.

James: Shit. I'm sorry.

Connor: It's okay. It is what it is, right? Can't change it, can't bring them back, so we've just gotta keep calm and carry on.

James: What was your dad like?

Connor: He was pretty cool. We used to do all the clichéd stuff; fish, play catch in the backyard, all that stuff.

James: They both died of cancer?

Connor: Yup. So if you're looking for someone with superior genes, I'm clearly not your guy.

James: Lol. I knew I forgot something in my bio.

Connor: Should we unmatch now? Save us both some heartache?

James: Probably. I mean, we can't have our kids having subpar genes.

Connor: Oh, we're having kids now?

I send the message with a heap of laughing faces so he knows I'm not running scared. It's not like kids are something that could just *happen* for me anyway, but the idea of being so happy and in love with someone that we want to raise kids together? I can't deny the fact the idea sounds more than attractive. But like, *years* from now.

Connor: James? Hello?

The message changes from *delivered* to *seen*. So I wait for his reply. And wait. Then wait some more.

I take a deep breath and decide to put him out of his misery.

Connor: In first grade I once shit my pants when I had to give a book report on *Ferdinand the Bull*.

James: Why on earth would you tell me that?

Connor: So we've both said something we never want people to know and can move on.

James: You're something else, you know that, right?

Connor: I am indeed aware.

James: Lol.

James: Thanks.

Connor: Don't mention it, and I mean that literally.

James: Mention what?

Connor: You catch on quick. I like that about you.

James: You like me, huh?

Connor: I dunno. Show me more of you than just your hand and I might change my mind.

A minute later a photo comes in of a golden torso, six-pack abs, a hand resting on the waistband of a pair of black basketball shorts, and a noticeable bulge below.

Connor: Wow.

James: You like?

Connor: Yeah. I like it a lot.

James: Your turn.

I take my shirt off and return the favor. I'm not as built as James is, but I can hold my own. Ever since I can remember, I've played baseball. First it was Little League, then I started playing in school—until I reached high school. It was always something Dad and I did together. Without him it didn't feel the same, so I stopped. But I have to admit, I miss it. Or is it being with my dad I miss?

James: Not bad.

The text interrupts my soul searching, thankfully, before I could get too deep and meaningful.

Connor: Yeah?

James: I'd do you.

I chuckle. Romance in the twenty-first century, ladies and gentlemen.

Connor: And just what would you do to me?

James: You're gonna play it like that?

Connor: Depends. Are you picking up what I've laid down?

James: First, I think I'd take those thick lips of yours and devour them. I bet you taste like whiskey and apple pie.

Connor: Whiskey and apple pie?

James: Two of my favorite things.

Connor: Fair enough. Proceed.

James: Thank you. As I was saying, I'd devour your

lips. **I'd kiss you so hard you'd be on the brink of coming just from that.**

I want to tell him I'm on the brink of coming *now* and he's not even touching me, but I think I've shared enough embarrassing confessions for today. My dick is so hard it's a wonder it hasn't punched a hole in my sweats. The boy has skills, I'll give him that.

Connor: Sounds good.

James: Just good?

Connor: I've got a feeling you know how good your skills are. You don't need me inflating your ego.

James: Is my ego the only thing getting bigger?

The message is accompanied by the smirking emoji. I chuckle and take a pic of my dick trying to escape my sweats.

Connor: Big enough for you?

He sends back the drooling emoji.

Connor: I want you to suck me so deep I hit the back of your throat.

James: Baby, I'd suck you so good you'll be lucky if you're able to function afterwards.

Connor: Promises, promises.

He sends me the lip licking emoji.

Connor: Am I the only one affected here?

In response, I get a shot of a very impressive boner, the tip poking out of those basketball shorts I was admiring before.

Connor: Glad to see I'm not alone.

James: Definitely not alone, but horny as fuck.

Connor: If I were there, I'd run my hand down your shaft, squeezing it, teasing you.

James: Mmm.

Connor: Are you doing it?

James: Yeah.

Connor: Good.

James: You?

Connor: Absolutely.

James: Good. Proceed.

I chuckle.

Connor: Now that you're good and primed, I'd use that drop of precum to help me run up and down, up and down. I'd roll your balls in my palms.

James: Would you suck them?

Connor: Do you want me to?

James: God, yes.

Connor: Then I'd suck them, before licking you all the way to your crown. I bet you taste salty, with just a hint of sweetness.

James: Keep going.

Connor: I'd suck you as deep as you're now sucking me, both of us racing to get each other off first.

James: Jesus, I'm close.

I switch my phone to record and film the last few strokes it takes before I'm coming all over my hand and stomach. I send it to him.

James: Shit, that's hot.

A second later, I get a photo of the mess he made all over himself.

Faintly I hear Amy call me for dinner, but I ignore her for the time being.

James: Looks like you made a mess of yourself.

Connor: Totally your fault

I clean myself up.

James: I'd say I'm sorry, but I'm not.

Connor: Lol. Neither am I.

"*Connor*," Amy yells, throwing my door open.

"Jesus fuck!" I cry, trying to cover myself up. "A little privacy?"

"I've been calling you for like, five minutes."

"And I've been busy."

"What? Watching porn? Is that really a good use of your time?"

"It's better than whatever you needed me for."

"Argh!" she yells. "Why do you do this, Connor? I'm doing my best to be civil to you, but why do you have to make everything so hard?"

"Because all of this, us trying to be a happy family, forgetting about the absolute shitshow of the past four years? Doesn't make it go away."

"I was nineteen."

"I was fourteen, barely a fucking teenager. I didn't get to run away. I didn't get to pretend everything was fine. I was there, every. Single. Day. I was there when Dad took his last breath. I watched Mom fall apart and then get sick herself. I saw her last breath too. I was the one who was there for Jase, raising him, taking care of him when our parents couldn't. I didn't get to pick and choose what I dealt with. I dealt with it *all*."

She throws her hands up. "When are we going to get past this? Every time we argue, it's the same thing over and over again. When are you going to forgive me?"

"When are you going to apologize?" I counter.

"I couldn't be there, Con," she says, tears in her eyes.

21

"And I can't be here." I get up and throw my shirt back on and slide into a pair of beat-up Vans, stuffing my phone and wallet in my pockets.

"Where are you going?" she asks as I brush past her.

"Anywhere but here."

I blow out of the apartment and rush down the stairs into the warm Chicago night. I walk with no destination in mind, just walk. My feet take me to the L, and when a train comes, I get on. Getting off once I reach downtown, I walk to the river, taking a seat on a bench.

My phone chirps in my pocket, and I realize James and what we just did is now nothing but a distant memory.

James: That was one hell of a get-to-know you.

James: I don't think I've come that hard in like, forever.

James: Is it clichéd if I ask if it was as good for you as it was for me?

James: Connor?

James: Hello?

James: So it wasn't as good for you as it was for me?

Connor: Sorry, shit hit the fan at home. I had to get out of there.

Connor: But yes, it definitely was as good for me as it was for you.

James: Everything ok?

Connor: Not even close.

Not long after I press send, my phone rings, James's number flashing up on the screen.

"H-Hey," I stammer.

"Hey, yourself," he replies, his voice rich and smooth.

"W-What's up?" I clear my throat in an attempt to get a grip on myself.

"Just wanted to hear your voice."

And statements like that aren't helping. "You did?" I've lost the stammer, but I'm afraid if my voice goes any higher, only dogs will hear me.

"You sounded like you were having a pretty shit time."

I chuckle. "Yeah, you could say that."

"Want to talk about it?"

"At this point, I've talked it over to death. Thanks for the offer though."

"If you did want to talk, or not, I'm here."

"Thanks."

There's a few moments of silence before I break it.

"So is there gonna be more chances for us to... not talk?" I ask.

"Is that your roundabout way of asking if there'll be more of us simultaneously masturbating?"

"That or, you know, *more*."

"More?" I can hear the smirk in his voice. The jerk is teasing me, and I don't altogether hate it. I don't know what that says about me, that I like his teasing, but right now, I don't care, I just want him to keep talking to me.

"Yeah, like in person."

"I dunno. School is about to start, and things are gonna be hectic for me."

"Oh, okay. No problem."

"It's not that I don't want to, I just.... My life is complicated as fuck right now, and I'm not sure I can take anything else on."

"It's totally fine, we'll just keep this casual, text or call when we can." I know his profile said nothing serious, but I can't help but thinking about the possibility of something more with him. He's a great listener, and he gets me. What's not to like about that?

"Yeah?"

I nod even though he can't see me. "Yeah. I mean, shit, it's my senior year and I'm about to start at a brand-new school. I'm sure my hands are going to be plenty full."

"I do like talking to you. A lot," he says.

"A lot, huh?"

He chuckles, and I realize I'm fishing for compliments.

"Yeah, a lot."

"Good."

"Smart-ass."

"Eh, you'll grow to love it."

"I don't doubt it."

"So, what's got your life so hectic?" I ask.

He blows out a breath. "A whole lot of shit."

"You can tell me if you want. I mean, it's only fair after I unloaded on you about my family."

"Man, this is some involved shit." He chuckles.

"I'm game."

"All right, but don't say I didn't warn you."

"Dude, I'm not some little bitch; hit me with the heavy stuff."

"So, my mom's in the public eye, like *majorly* in the public eye. It feels like she has been since I was born. Because of that, she has certain... expectations."

"Right."

"My dad, on the other hand, is less involved. I don't know if it's lack of ambition on his part or if he's just happy for her to have the spotlight. Either way, he lets her do her own thing, which basically means she controls everything and no one is allowed to disagree with her."

"And you disagree," I guess.

He gives a wry chuckle. "Yeah, just a bit."

"She gives you a hard time?"

"A hard time I could handle. She's a tyrant."

"Does she know about your, um, sexual orientation?"

"Nah, or if she does, she ignores it and is hoping I grow out of it. Any vagina she deems 'worthy,' she pushes at me. Every chance she gets."

"Oof."

"Yeah."

"But you obviously don't care about that, about them."

"Oh, I don't care about them, but that doesn't mean I don't 'do my duty' and make it seem like I do."

"Dude...."

"It's the life I lead."

"It, um, sounds kind of horrific."

"I know it sounds bad, but what else can I do? If I want to keep them off my back, then I have to play the role."

"When you put it that way...," I say. In truth, I have no idea what I would do in the same position. My parents were great when I came out to them, and, well, I don't really give a fuck what Amy thinks.

"So you've never had a relationship you've wanted?"

"Not really. I mean, there was one guy but we... it... My life isn't easy."

"I'm so sorry, James."

"It is what it is, right?"

"What happened with you and him?"

"An ending Shakespeare would be proud of."

"Wow."

"Life with me is fun."

"That's certainly been my experience."

He snorts. "Yeah, on the other end of the phone."

"Does that diminish it?"

"It's certainly not the full experience."

"Maybe I'm just getting the good bits at the moment. I'm more than okay with that."

"Some would say there are no good bits with me."

"And I'm here to tell them otherwise."

"You sweet-talker you."

"Is this where I say 'aww, shucks'?" I ask.

He chuckles again. "Yeah, something like that."

"It's only for one more year, though. I mean, you're a senior, so you'll be going to college next year, won't you?"

"College is a whole other thing. I want to get the fuck away from here, but my mom…."

"Let me guess. She wants you to go to her alma mater and I'm gonna go with prelaw."

"Got it in one."

"And you?"

"I want to sit on a beach somewhere, running a bar nearby with a hot man to suck my dick anytime I want."

"Sounds like a dream."

"And that's all it'll be."

"You never told me which school you go to. It's not Windswept by any chance?" Yes, I know he told me not ten minutes ago there's no room in his life for me, but a boy can hope, can't he?

"Afraid you're not that lucky, champ. It's Victorious for me."

He names one of Chicago's other elite high schools.

"Oh. Oh well."

"Nervous about starting?"

"Nah." I try to brush it off. "School is school, right? It's the same everywhere."

"Keep telling yourself that. This is Chicago."

"Meaning?"

"You're in the big city now. Things here aren't the same as bumfuck Wisconsin—"

"Michigan," I correct.

"Whatever. You're in the big leagues now."

"Seriously? How different can it be?"

"Look, obviously I don't know what your old school was like and I care even less about it, but Windswept…." He blows out a breath. "Cavanaugh McLaughlin rules Windswept. You know the type. Good-looking, cocky, brash, ego the size of Texas. Anything he wants, he gets. No one questions him. No one challenges him. And let's not forget about his faithful band of minions. Naturally, they all worship the ground he walks on. If he decides he doesn't like you, he will eat you alive."

I scoff. "Please, this guy's what? Eighteen? How much can he get away with?"

"You'd be surprised. His parents have got the faculty on lockdown, so they let him get away with *everything*."

"Then I guess I'll just have to stay on his good side then." Trouble is the last thing I want. This year, all I want is to put my head down, do my work, and get out of there. Get out of *here*.

"I'd advise it. The last guy who didn't.... It didn't end well for him."

"Is this what you were telling me about a while ago? Didn't he die or something?"

"Rumor has it that *Cav* did it."

"And how much stock do we put in this rumor?" I ask.

"As much as you want, I suppose. One thing that is true is that Cav was there when he died."

"There's a big difference between being in the vicinity when someone died and being responsible for it." Having been the subject of many a high school rumor, I've learned you have to take them with more than a grain of salt. When someone says he was "there" it could mean anything from he was in the room, to he was somewhere in the vicinity, or not even there at all. Besides, I like to give the benefit of the doubt; it's what I'd want someone to do for me.

"Look at you, sucking up to Cav and you haven't even met him yet. You'll fit in *just* fine."

I roll my eyes even though he can't see them. "I just don't put stock in bullshit rumors probably started by some pseudo straight guy who wants Cav's dick in his ass."

James laughs. "What the fuck are you on about?"

I lean back against the hard bench. "It's my experience that rumors such as that are started, 99 percent of the time, by someone who's got a hard-on for the subject."

"And just how many rumors are these results based on?"

"A lot."

"Oh, *that* many, huh?"

28

"Yeah, that many."

We both laugh.

"I'm just saying that until I hear for myself what happened, I'm going to reserve judgment. There's two sides to every story, and holy fuck."

"What? What's wrong?" he asks.

"I just realized exactly how big of a jackass I've been to my sister."

He laughs. "Is that all?"

"Seriously, I've been horrible."

"Does she deserve it?"

"Maybe, but also maybe not."

"Ah, come on, you know she does. You wouldn't have thought it in the first place if you didn't."

"Maybe I was angry and taking it out on her."

"Or maybe she actually deserved it."

I blow out a breath and run my hand through my hair. "And I suppose Cavanaugh McLaughlin deserves everything he gets too?"

"Yeah, he does. Connor...," he starts.

"Yeah?" I ask when he doesn't continue.

"Just be careful around him. Staying away would be even better. He's.... He's not a nice guy."

"Are you trying to look out for me, James? If I were a different type of guy, I might mistake that for caring."

He chuckles. "Ask anyone who knows me and they'll tell you that's the least likely thing coming from me."

"Hmm, I don't know. I think under that brash exterior is someone I'd very much like to get to know, if you'd let me."

CHAPTER 4

W indswept Academy is everything I thought it
would be. Set on sprawling, manicured grounds,
the driveway has to be at least half a mile long. I guess it's
building the anticipation so when you finally see the
imposing five-story sandstone building you're sufficiently
awed. To me, it looks like just another stuck-up prep
school. These places are nothing but a waste of money
designed to make parents feels as if they're giving their
offspring the best opportunity at a future they'd be proud
of, but which the kids couldn't give a flying fuck about.

As we draw closer, the school looms large. Ivy covers
one of the walls and some of the front, making it the most
clichéd building ever.

"Ugh," I say.

"I think it looks fancy," Jase says.

I roll my eyes. "It looks like it has a giant stick up its
pretentious ass."

"Mom and Dad specifically outlined in their wills that

if you moved to Chicago, this is where you were to go," Amy says from the driver seat of her SUV.

"Because you're so good at following their wishes," I mutter under my breath.

She sighs. I guess I'm getting a little predictable in my comebacks.

"At least you're only here for a year," Jase grumbles.

I twist in my seat to face him. "Hey, you're going to love it here. I bet you fit right in and make a ton of friends."

"Why can't you be that positive with your own life?" Amy asks.

"Because, unlike me, he's still got his entire high school career in front of him. I don't. This is my senior year. You remember what that entails, right?"

She shakes her head as she pulls to a stop. "I'll be here at three thirty to pick you guys up," she says.

"How motherly of you," I retort, gathering my bag that's at my feet.

Amy whirls to face me, her boring brown hair, so much like my own, flying everywhere. "Do you have a better suggestion?"

"I don't know, Amy, maybe a car of my own? I am seventeen, legally old enough to drive, you know. Plus, think of all the time it'll free up for you if you don't have to worry about driving me and Jase everywhere. I mean, you'd be the real winner here, and we know that's all that matters. Besides, I have my own money Mom and Dad left me."

"That you can't touch without my approval," she reminds me. "But," she continues before I can mount another argument, "let's see how this week goes, okay? Yes, you having a car would be handy, but I'm not going to reward you, especially given your behavior lately."

I try to hide my smile. "I'll be on my best behavior."

The words have no sooner left my mouth when a monster, an absolute dream of a car, pulls into the student lot. The exhaust is so loud it drowns everything else out. The 1970 Chevy Chevelle SS is the stuff of legends. Mom and I dreamed of getting our hands on one and doing it up. Her dad used to work for Chevy and would tell her all about them every night when he came home from the factory.

The Chevelle in question is a beauty, but in a lot full of Ferraris, Aston Martins, and even a Bugatti, it's a little out of place.

"Did you see that?" Jase asks. Even if I couldn't see his face, the amount of wonder in his voice is hard to ignore.

"Mmm-hmm. She's a beauty."

Amy shakes her head. "Best behavior." She points at me. "Prove to me you can be a decent human being, and we'll talk."

"If I do, can I get one of those?" I nod to the red beauty.

"No."

"But—"

"I may not share your and Mom's love for cars but even I can tell that that car is something you should not be in charge of."

The retort on my lips disappears when the driver gets out. He's hot, but much like his car, he doesn't seem like your stereotypical elite private school boy. Actually, "boy"

33

is probably the wrong word. "Guy" or "man" is more accurate, and boy is he *all* man.

Tall—I'm going to go with six foot two, six foot three—with short sandy-brownish hair, a solid body that is obviously worked for, and good Lord. I have to stop myself swooning as he rolls the sleeves of his white Windswept shirt up, revealing two full arms of tattoos. I'm not sure how one gets away with that, but I'm guessing a decent amount of cash, or perhaps a new library, has to change hands.

"Wow," Jase whispers.

"Yup."

"I'll be back at three thirty," Amy reminds us. "Behave and have a good day."

I give her a salute before I shut the car door, and she drives off.

"Are you really going to try and get a car?" Jase asks as we stand on the sidewalk, my eyes still fixed on the hunk with the Chevelle.

"I said so, didn't I?"

He shrugs. "You say a lot of things."

I hook an arm around his neck and steer him toward the school. "Could you imagine taking a spin in that?" I nod back to the red beauty.

"The car or the guy?" Jase asks, his signature cheeky grin on his face.

I give him a shove but bring him back to me pretty quickly.

"Out of my way, pretty boy," a behemoth says as he shoves his way between my brother and me.

"Ugh, rude." I sigh, but keep on walking. I don't want

any trouble here, I just want to do what I need to do in order to get out of here.

From behind us, he chuckles. I turn to face him.

He's tall, maybe a little taller than the Chevelle hunk. I'm going with six foot four, six foot five, with long blond hair that flops over his brows and the brownest eyes I've ever seen. I'm seriously starting to wonder if being ridiculously good-looking is a prerequisite for admission here.

"Is there a problem here?" he asks.

I hold my hands up. "Nope, no problem. Just, maybe, look where you're walking?"

He shrugs. "You were in my way."

"Possibly, but there's plenty of space out here, I'm sure you could've walked around. But," I say before he can interject, "it's fine, we're totally cool. Just be careful next time."

He laughs. "Look, pretty boy, I'm not sure where the fuck you came from, nor do I care, but you're at Windswept now. I don't give a fuck who you are, but you're under our rules now, and our rules say that if you're in my way, I'm going to take you out of it."

I hold up my hands again. "Hey, no harm, no foul. I'm new here and don't want any trouble." Normally guys like this would drive me mad thinking they're better than everyone else but.... I blow out a breath. I don't want any trouble. The more I say it, the greater the likelihood I'll be able to stick to it.

"Let's go, Con," Jase say quietly, tugging my arm.

The guy with the Chevelle walks around in front of

me, pausing for a second, assessing me before asking the blond, "What's the issue here?"

"I'm just letting pretty boy Con here know the way the world works."

He nods.

"Look," I say, "we just want to get inside. We didn't mean any harm or want to cause any trouble."

"I'd say that's a good thing," the Chevelle hunk says.

I nod. "It won't be a problem."

"Hmm." He grabs my chin, his blue eyes piercing mine, looking for I don't know what. He lets my face go. "Stay the fuck out of my way."

"Like I said, that won't be a problem."

"Good." He pushes past us and walks toward the building.

"Stay cool, little Con," the blond pit bull says, slamming into my shoulder yet again when he walks past.

"Those guys are dicks," Jase says once they're gone.

"Mmm," I agree. But that doesn't mean I don't want to fuck one or both.

CHAPTER 5

I'm sure the faculty and donors who support Windswept Academy would like to think it's far superior to every other elite private school in the country, but I hate to break it to them; it's not. Don't get me wrong, the building and all the shit in it is very nice, but at the end of the day, it's just a school. Sure, the marble floors and built-in oak lockers with electronic locks are nice, but I suspect there would be other schools across the nation with similar, if not the same, facilities.

The uniform of dark gray slacks and a white button-up shirt for the guys, gray pleated skirt and white blouse for the girls, is one I could've predicted before Amy dumped the ensemble on my bed the other night. What's also expected is the short skirt lengths, tight blouses exposing every color bra under the sun, and more rolled-up shirtsleeves than a political conference in Hawaii.

But I guess it's not *too* bad. The student body seems attractive enough, not forgetting the two from outside whom, despite their holier-than-thou attitudes, I'd still like to climb like trees.

James's warning about Cavanaugh McLaughlin is also at the forefront of my mind. I know he said he doesn't have time for a relationship, but that warning, that was him showing concern, right? It was him not wanting me to get involved with someone who's clearly bad news. That has to mean something, doesn't it? I mean, you wouldn't tell someone to stay away from trouble if you didn't care, would you?

I walk with Jase to the office to get our schedules and IDs.

"You think you'll be okay?" I ask him as we stand outside the office.

He rolls his eyes. "I'll be fine, Con."

I ruffle his hair. "You know I worry about you."

"But you don't need to. I can handle myself."

I nod and take a breath. "Yeah, I know. Old habits and all that."

"I'll be fine," he reiterates. "*If* I need anything, I'll call or text or send a carrier pigeon."

"Very funny," I say as I give him a playful shove. "Get to class, and I'll see you at three thirty."

Jase goes right, while I go left, heading to my first class, English.

The class has already started by the time I get there, ensuring the awkward interruption. Thankfully, I'm not made to do the typical new student introduction and am sent to a seat at a table with a blonde bombshell, despite a whole other empty desk being available. But, being the good boy I am, I take the seat I'm directed to.

If I swung that way, I'd totally do her. As it is, it doesn't stop me from checking her out. She has long blonde hair, with one half of her head shaved. Her moss-green eyes are heavily lined with eyeliner and coated generously in mascara. Classic red lipstick is painted on her pouty lips that snarl at me when she sees me checking her out. She crosses her arms over a very generous chest, her blouse unbuttoned to where the cups of her black lace bra meet.

"Don't even think about it," she says as I sit down, her voice rough around the edges.

I chuckle as I sit down. "Don't think about what, sweetheart?"

"About figuring out how best to get in my panties. I'm telling you right now, you're not my type."

I lean in, right up to her ear. "I'm *everyone's* type." Even though I have zero desire to do anything with this girl, it's still amusing as fuck to play with her a bit.

She shakes her head.

"Tell me, princess." I pick up a lock of her hair and twirl it around my finger. "What makes you think I want you, anyway?"

"Your obvious hard…" She trails off as her eyes dip to my flat slacks.

"You mean the hard-on I *don't* have for you?" I ask.

She swallows. "Er…."

I lean back. "Don't worry about it, darlin', you're not my type either."

She twists to face me, eyebrow cocked.

"While I very much appreciate the package, you're missing one *very* big one," I say, my eyes directed between her legs.

"Really?" She leans forward, her tits almost falling out of her top.

I shrug. "I know it's a waste, but a guy's gotta do what a guy's gotta do."

"I get that," she says, leaning back in her seat.

I put out my hand. "Connor Siddell."

She takes what I'm offering her. "Chloe Fantana."

"Well, Chloe Fantana, I guess this means we can be wastes together."

She shoots me a blinding smile.

"It's a pity though; we would've made one hot couple."

"That we would," she agrees, pulling my arm around her back so it rests on the top of her seat. I raise my eyebrows.

"I figure it'll give 'em something to talk about." She nods to the rest of the class, most of whose attention is on us.

"Still in?" I ask.

"No, I just like to keep 'em guessing. You'll learn pretty quickly at this school, everyone thinks they know everyone else. You're pigeonholed by who your family is, or how much they're worth, or how powerful they are. I don't subscribe to that theory. My parents take every opportunity to disown me, so why should who they are dictate how other people perceive me? I'm my own person. It's not my fault these lemmings don't have an original thought in their tiny brains. But you, you're going to fuck shit up with those dreamy eyes and that perfect hair. The girls are all going to want you, and I want to a) be the first one to call dibs, in doing so confusing their narrow minds, and b) have a front-row seat to their heartbreak when they find out you're not interested in them anyway."

I chuckle and slide closer to her. She smells like cotton candy. "Well then, it sounds like you and me are gonna have some fun around here."

"Stick with me, kid, and we'll have them eating out of the palms of our hands."

Before I know what's happening, she grabs my face and smacks a kiss on my lips. There are gasps from the other students in the class, but all that is forgotten when the door to the classroom is flung open, smashing into the wall behind it. The Chevelle guy from the parking lot stares right at me, his trusty sidekick by his side.

I muffle a groan and slide down in my seat.

Chloe chuckles and shakes her head. "Already had a run-in with the bad boys of Windswept Academy, have we?" she asks.

"You could say that."

She chuckles again.

"Mr. McLaughlin," the teacher says, breaking our bubble. "How nice of you to join us. You too, Mr. Rose."

The sidekick, Rose, turns and walks to the empty desk while McLaughlin continues to stare at me. I have no idea what his problem is, but the attention isn't completely unwanted, despite my pledge to be good this year. There's something about him that is... intriguing to me.

"Don't even think about it," Chloe says, hand resting on my shoulder, lips at my ear. "Cav will eat you alive."

"Cav?" I ask, turning to face her and breaking the connection I had with him.

"Yeah, Cavanaugh McLaughlin and his lackey, Thomas

Rose. Cav's the all-round badass and supreme leader of Windswept Academy."

"And why do I want to stay clear of a fine specimen such as that?" I ask, James's warning ringing loud and clear in my mind.

"He's bad news," Chloe says. "Ignoring the fact he's supposed to have killed Max Emory last summer, he's a mean son of a bitch who delights in tormenting others. He gets off on it. In my unprofessional opinion, he's bordering on psychopathic. Just leave it, Connor. He might be all kinds of pretty and tempting, but that is one guy you don't want to fuck with."

As she says this, Thomas walks past our desk. "You've got a little..." He points to the corner of his mouth. Chloe looks over and wipes away some of the lipstick she left when she kissed me.

Meanwhile Cav continues on to his seat next to his sidekick. Even though I don't turn around, I can feel his eyes on me, burning into the side of my head. The warnings about this guy are piling up, but something is pulling me to him, something I'm not sure I want to fight.

CHAPTER 6

"So tell me," I say to Chloe as we sit in the cafeteria. "How does a nice girl like you end up kissing strange guys minutes after meeting them?" Although, we're fast friends now, having shared another class since then.

She shrugs and pops a fry in her mouth. "Just lucky, I guess."

I stare at her until she gives in with a sigh.

"Ugh, *fine*. So, it's no secret that dudes don't do it for me. I told you earlier my parents are still and probably always will be in denial about that fact."

"That sucks. I'm sorry," I tell her. I guess I lucked out in a big way with the fact my parents took my sexual orientation in their stride.

She waves me off. "It is what it is. Growing up, I knew they'd never accept it."

"Okay…," I prompt, not quite sure how this has anything to do with what I asked.

"But I thought, I *hoped*, the kids that went here, that I've known basically my whole life, would be different. I hoped they could see through all the bullshit our parents spewed, that they'd hear it and laugh, tell them they're being old fuddy-duddies or whatever."

"And they didn't."

She shakes her head. "No, they didn't. Instead, they lap up whatever their parents tell them, questioning nothing."

"Hardly fills you with confidence, does it?" I ask.

She laughs halfheartedly. "No, it doesn't."

"So all of this," I wave a hand up and down her body, "is to what? Keep them on their toes? Keep them guessing?"

"That, and to show them what they'll never have."

I raise an eyebrow. "*No* one here has caught your eye?" I ask. "Actually, fuck that, no one here has tried to fuck you?"

Her face darkens, jaw clenching. "They've tried. Boy, have they tried. I think some of the girls are legitimately curious, and I will admit I have dabbled with some of them. They like to think they're badass. I like to think I've turned them. Neither statement is particularly true. All of that is child's play compared to the guys, though."

"Have they…?"

She nods. "Many and often."

"Holy fuck."

She shrugs. "I'm unnatural, you see, against the natural order. Women are there to be at a man's side, and one as hot as me? It's inconceivable I *wouldn't* be interested in one of them. And maybe I just haven't had the right one."

"Please tell me no one actually said that."

She snorts. "I've lost count of the number of times I've heard it."

"So kissing me was—"

"A big fuck-you to everyone," she finishes for me. "I want to show them all what they can't have."

"Um, that's great and all, and I love you want to fuck with the entire student body, but I'm very much out of the closet and don't intend on going back in it here."

She shrugs. "Who says you have to? We can fuck with their heads a bit, can't we? Keep them guessing?"

I think back to my run-in with Cav and his pit bull this morning. I don't want trouble, but a little bit of fun never hurt anyone, right? Besides, I have to do something to keep this year even the slightest bit interesting. "A little bit of fuckery *might* be amusing."

She raises an eyebrow. "Might?"

"Okay, more than might," I concede.

She nods. "That's what I thought."

"So there's no one here who's catching your eye?" I ask.

"Not really. I'm content to be a free woman for the time being."

"You never know...."

She gasps. "Connor Siddell, are you a *romantic?*"

I chuckle and shrug. "You got me."

She laughs. "Well, I'll be damned."

"There's nothing wrong with a little romance," I tell her.

"No, I guess there's not. Maybe I'm just pessimistic."

I grab her hand. "Well, now you've got me to balance that out."

She gives me that stunning smile again. "Yeah, I guess I do."

"We're going to be great friends, you and I."

The rest of the day goes relatively smoothly. I don't have any more classes with Cavanaugh, but I do have physics and gym with Thomas. It seems, however, that when his master's not around, he doesn't have the balls to go after me. Instead, he hangs around with some of the guys I saw him with at lunch. It's a predictable group of generally good-looking guys all with massive egos inflated by the knowledge they're basically untouchable. It's the same attitude guys across the country have, I'm sure, but here... it feels different, like these guys mean more, can get away with more, as stupid as it sounds.

Chloe finds me before the day is through to check in before kissing me and strutting away.

"Holy fuck," Jase says. "Who's the hottie?"

"Chloe."

"Is Chloe in need of a boyfriend?" he asks.

I slap him on the back of the head. "One, she's gay and doesn't want your scrawny ass, and two, she is my friend and deserves respect."

He rolls his eyes. "And I was simply respecting her fine physical appearance."

I shove a few books I don't need into my locker before shutting it. "Come on, Amy's waiting on us."

Jase walks by my side as we navigate our way out of the building.

"As much as I like Amy driving us, I can't wait for you to have your own car," he says.

"Yeah?" I ask.

He nods.

"You gonna help me do it up when she finally lets me get one?"

"She will. I bet she hates having to drop us off and pick us up as much as we do."

"Let's hope so," I say as we walk down the front steps.

Cavanaugh, Thomas, and their bunch of merry men are at the bottom, holding court, eyeing everyone as they leave.

"Did he give you a hard time today?" Jase asks as we walk past.

My head whips to face him. "You worried about me, kid?" I ask.

He shrugs. "You're my brother."

"Yeah, your *older* brother."

"Who has spent more than his fair share of time worrying about me. I'm returning the favor."

I shoot him a smile.

"Plus, if you get in trouble, Amy won't let you get a car."

I shove him, laughing as I do. "That's all you want me for, to be your personal chauffeur, huh?"

"If the opportunity presents itself." He looks back over his shoulder toward Cavanaugh. "Just be careful, okay, Con? I have a bad feeling about that guy."

I sling my arm around Jase's neck and kiss the top of his head. I spare my own glance back at Cavanaugh, finding his eyes on me.

The warnings about this guy are mounting, but there's something about him that doesn't want me to let go.

CHAPTER 7

After two weeks at Windswept Academy, it's clear to me the rumors of Cavanaugh McLaughlin's powers weren't exaggerated. There's no doubting he's the big man on campus, that he rules the school. He's untouchable, both physically and metaphorically. No one goes near him save for Thomas and his band of merry men. He lives in a bubble here, held above everyone else, present only because he has to be. But I don't buy it. He gives off this unaffected air, but it's too cultivated, too smooth. Several times over the past two weeks, I've watched him. I can't help it. My eyes are drawn to him. But I've vowed that's all I'll do, look. So I do. I've watched how his smile doesn't reach his eyes, how he chuckles, not laughs, how he clenches his fists and grits his teeth when his friends are being idiots. This act, or whatever it is he's putting on, is wearing on him. I can see it, clear as day. Which makes me wonder, why can't anyone else? The mystery that is Cavanaugh McLaughlin has got me more than fascinated.

"You're staring at him again," Chloe says as we eat lunch.

"I am not," I rebut, not tearing my eyes away from him.

"Uh-huh, so why are you looking in his direction?"

"There's something interesting on the wall over there."

"It's a smudge."

"Well, it's very… artistic."

She snorts and throws a tater tot at my head. I finally tear my eyes away from Cavanaugh.

"Oh look, there he is."

I give her the finger. Over the past few weeks, we've developed what I hope is a firm and lasting friendship. She's a hoot to be around, always keeping things interesting, not giving a fuck what people think. And I have to admit, it's been more than a bit fun keeping people on their toes trying to guess what the hell we're up to. I'm not hiding my sexuality, but at the same time, I'm not flaunting it either.

"I don't know what your obsession with him is, but you need to forget about him Con. He's dangerous and not the type of guy you want to have anything to do with."

"I know, I know. But I can't help it. Since before I got here, all I've been hearing about is how I need to stay away from him. He's bad, he's scary, he's not a nice guy, but so far, I've seen none of that. Okay, he's not the friendliest guy, but I get that. He has a rep to protect. But I think there's more to him."

She shakes her head. "You're hopeless."

I nod. "Yes, I am." I chuckle. "Look, I'm not going to do anything. The last thing I want is to cause trouble, there's just something about him."

She rolls her eyes.

"I just don't get why everyone says he's so bad. Surely for a guy as good-looking as that one, all sins are forgivable?"

"Even murder?"

I put my fork down. "I've heard about this so-called murder but I've not heard any details, which frankly makes me question its legitimacy."

Chloe snickers. "Frankly you question its legitimacy?" she asks. "Sorry, counselor, I didn't realize I had to meet a specific burden of proof."

"Now look who's being fancy." I throw a piece of cantaloupe at her. "But seriously, what happened?"

"To be honest, I don't think there's much to the rumor, that it's just that, a rumor. There's probably *some* truth to it, but I think there's also a lot of hot air being blown, all designed to make Cav look like a badder ass than he already is."

"If you don't believe it, then why does it keep coming up?" I ask.

She shrugs. "Because all the lackeys here want to suck up to Cav, to make themselves feel better when he doesn't give them the time of day? I don't know. I think they've just bought into this... idea of who Cav is and no one really questions it."

"You know how stupid that sounds, right?"

She throws another tater tot at me. "Of course I do, but when you're the only one who doesn't give a shit, well, it's easier just to go along with things."

I shake my head. "One thing I don't understand—"

"Just one?" she asks, poking her tongue out.

It's my turn to throw a tot. "—is why he's content to have a rumor about him being a murderer. That's just… crazy to me."

"Okay, you might have a point there."

"Right? I mean, why on earth would you think that's a *good* thing?"

She shrugs. "Maybe it's to keep all the annoying blowflies that litter this place, away. You know, if they think he killed someone, then they'll be too scared to try and be friends with him."

"Hmm, that could work."

"I mean, if that's what it took for people to leave *me* alone I'd totally consider it."

I give her a look.

"What?"

"You'd really be happy to be known as a murderer?"

"It's not like I actually *did* the act, just have enough doubt and intrigue surrounding it so that people wouldn't bother me anymore."

"Is it really that bad?" I ask.

"Yes and no. It's nothing I can't handle, but then, is it really something I should have to handle?"

I grab her hand and give it a squeeze. "No, it's not."

The bell rings and I get up.

She grabs my arm. "But I am serious about Cav though. Stay away from him. I know he's all kinds of pretty but he's not someone you want to mess with. Even if he's not responsible for Max's death, he can still make your life a living nightmare and I don't want that for you."

I bend down and kiss her cheek. "You're a real sweetheart, you know that?"

She shoves me away, but not as hard as she normally would. "Don't tell anyone."

I mime zipping my lips shut. "It'll be our secret."

As I say that, a shoulder barges into me, pushing me back a foot or so.

"If you think you've got a chance with that one, you're dumber than I thought," Cav snarls.

"Spending time with a beautiful woman is never a waste of time," I tell him.

"You know you're not her type, don't you?"

"I do, but I don't see how it's your concern." I really don't either. Why is he worried about me and Chloe spending time together? He doesn't want her and he sure as shit doesn't want me, even if I would say yes.

"No concern," he says.

"Okay, then. Nice talking to you?"

He gives me a shove as he walks past.

"What was that about?" Chloe asks.

"I have absolutely no idea."

She tilts her head.

"What?" I ask.

She shakes her head. "Nothing, that was just super weird."

I hold my hands up. "I didn't do anything." No matter how much I wanted to.

"Hmm."

I don't know what I did to attract Cav's notice, and as much as I said I'll not get involved with all things him, I can't help but get a thrill from his attention on me.

. . .

"So how's school going?" James asks me as I lie on my bed later that night. As he foreshadowed, we haven't been able to talk much since school went back, but the stars aligned for us to talk tonight.

"It's school. You go, you learn things, you talk shit, you go home."

He laughs, and I try not to think about what the sound does to my insides.

"So no run-ins with Cav then?"

"Cav who?" I ask.

"Connor...."

"James...."

"Cav's not somebody you should be playing with."

"Hey! I'm trying to be good, but we keep... running into each other."

"You need to leave him alone."

"I'm trying! But I can't help it if he doesn't want to cooperate."

He groans. "Just stay away from him, Connor. Please, for me."

"You know, that's a very boyfriend-y thing to say." The words are out of my mouth before I even realize what I've said. "I mean.... Uh...."

"I've gotta go," he blurts out.

"James, wa—"

"Just stay away from Cav, okay?"

I don't have time to reply as he ends the call.

"Fuck!"

CHAPTER 8

The Mustang R-SPEC is a beautiful car. It's the most potent, performance-focused Mustang ever and is an individually numbered, limited edition piece of American muscle.

And number thirteen, in a beautiful Velocity Blue, is all mine.

"How...?" I manage to choke out.

Amy shrugs while Jase bounces up and down.

"I've seen the effort you've been putting in this past month, and it is your eighteenth birthday, so I asked Jase what car he thought you'd want." She stops and swallows. "It also might be an apology, not that I can apologize enough, about how the past few years have gone and, ah, my, um, you know, not really being there."

I nod.

"But this doesn't mean you can go off the rails again, okay?"

"Yeah, okay," I reply, giving her a smile.

"Go on." She hands me the keys.

I run around to the driver side while Jase jumps in the passenger side.

I lower his window and lean over him to talk to her. "You don't want to come?"

She waves a hand. "You guys go and have fun, but, ah, try to stick to the state, okay?"

"Who wants to go to Wisconsin anyway?" Jase asks.

"Go!" she says again as I start the car, the engine purring.

At the sound, Jase and I look at each other, massive smiles on our faces.

"This car…."

"She wanted to get you something you'd like."

I run my hands over the steering wheel. "I'm not saying this makes up for her not being with us through everything, but it *does* help. A bit."

"She is trying, Con."

"I know, I just can't…. It's hard."

I spare him a glance, and he nods.

I blow out a breath. "But I'll try, okay?"

"Good."

"I mean, a car like this deserves some effort, right?"

"Definitely."

"Want to see what it can do?" I ask, taking the turn that will lead us to the freeway.

"Let's do it!"

The car drives like a dream, as you would expect, and pulling into the student parking lot on

Monday, I know there are a lot of eyes on it—and me, once I park and get out.

"Oooh, fancy," Chloe says, coming over to us.

"It's not fancy," I tell her. "It's a goddamn work of art, a limited edition of the most potent Mustang *ever*."

"All right, all right. Are you going to drive it or fuck it?"

"He's going to look like a pussy when it's left in the dust," Cav says, shutting the door of his Chevelle.

I chuckle and shake my head.

"Seriously," he says, "you think your car has anything on mine?"

I shrug. I'm not going to engage him on this. I *will* not engage. Even though he's dead wrong and I would die to see my car up against his. The sheer amount of horsepower that would be involved in that race... It would be a car lover's wet dream, all their Christmases come at once.

"This is the car of cars, a dream, an enigma, a goddamn fucking unicorn. Your shiny, fresh-off-the-assembly-line tin can might look good, but that's all it does. You know it, I know it, they know it." He nods to the gathered crowd.

He steps closer to me, his rich, woodsy scent with a hint of engine oil invading my senses. "You think you can show me up, boy? In *my* own school? It was a sweet effort, but in the end, it's going to fall embarrassingly short for you. I restored this car with my own hands. Hour upon hour of my blood, sweat, and tears has gone into this car. You think you can challenge me with something that just rolled off the showroom floor?" He laughs and pats my cheek. "Good try, but not good enough," he says before walking off.

"I wasn't trying to show you up," I say, even though he's far enough away that he can't hear me.

"Oof," Chloe says as she heads toward the school building as well.

"Dude...," Jase says.

"I didn't do anything!" I say. "I *never* do anything but that doesn't seem to register with anyone. This is all him!"

"And you're not interested in him?" Jase asks.

"Of course I'm not."

He looks at me.

"Okay, fine, he's good-looking, but that's it. The guy is an A-grade bully. I'm just trying to get through my senior year so I can get out of here."

"Out of here?" Jase asks, his voice strangled.

"Shit. I mean—"

"It's okay, I get it."

"Jase," I grab his arm as he turns to walk away. "I didn't mean it like that. I just...."

"You want to be somewhere where you can forget about everything."

"I just want to be normal," I tell him.

He gives me a sad smile. "I hate to tell you, but you'll never be normal."

I sigh.

"I just... miss them, so much."

Jase throws his arm around my shoulders. "I know. Me too."

"Mom would've loved this car, wouldn't she?"

He nods. "I think you would've been lucky to have it to yourself. She'd be asking to borrow it on a daily basis."

I laugh.

"It's a great car."

"It is."

"I should be nicer to Amy for it."

"You should. You should be nicer to everyone."

"I *am* nice! It's other people who aren't nice to *me*."

He rolls his eyes.

"What? It's true."

"Yeah, okay."

"I'm trying to be good," I tell him. Cav might be getting his digs in, but I won't react.

"Good, keep doing that."

"I will."

"But what he said about the Mustang not being able to keep up with his Chevelle? Dead wrong."

I manage a smile. "Thanks, kid." I sling my arm around his neck. "You're a good one, you know that?"

"It's because I have an awesome big brother to look up to."

My phone ringing drags me from the hell that is my calculus homework.

"I didn't think I'd hear from you again," I say in greeting.

James chuckles. "Yeah, sorry about that. I was a dick."

"Good thing I happen to like dicks then, isn't it?"

"I guess it is."

I sigh and run my hand through my hair. "Let's just forget that whole conversation ever happened."

"Sounds good to me. How was your day?" he asks.

"Ha! Pretty shitty, actually."

"Oh, sorry."

"It's fine, I'm just having a sort of hard time at school and I want to forget all about it." Even if Cav's blue-gray eyes are proving to be impossible to forget about.

"Cav causing problems?" he asks.

"Can we not talk about Cav?"

"That is absolutely not a problem. In fact, if you remember correctly, I've been asking not to talk about him for ages."

"Okay, smart-ass."

"You'd love to take my smart ass."

"Fuck yeah, I would," I reply, my dick jerking to life in my shorts.

"Would you bend me over? Take me from behind? Tower over me, feeling like you own me?"

"You'd like that, wouldn't you?" I counter. "Being completely at my mercy, my fingers in your ass, teasing your prostate, stretching you, filling you."

He groans, and just like that I go from half to full mast.

"I want to see you," I moan, freeing my erection and giving it a tug.

"How's that?" he asks.

I pull the phone away from my ear and see a tanned body and a hard dick.

"*So* much better," I say, switching the camera around so it shows the same thing.

"I want to watch you," he tells me.

"Yeah? You get off on me getting off?" I give myself a squeeze.

"Fuck."

I stroke myself again.

"Yeah, that's it," he encourages.

I milk myself, a drop of precum beading at my tip, and use it to give myself some lubrication.

"Look at what you're doing to me," I tell him.

He chuckles. "Yeah? It's a two-way street, buddy." He runs his thumb over his crown, collecting his own drop of precum. That star-shaped scar is stark against his tan skin.

"I bet you'd feel good in my hand. Long and hard and thick."

"Fuck yeah, I would," he replies.

"I'd take us in my hand, jerking us both, bringing us close so I could feel your skin against mine."

"Mmm," he moans.

"Do you like that?" I ask. "Want that?"

He arches his back, thrusting into his palm harder, faster. "Yes," he breathes.

I match my pace with his.

"But that's not where you want me, is it?"

"No."

"You want me in your ass. Your hot, tight ass."

"Yes, that's where I want you," he groans.

"You want me thrusting into you, grabbing your hips and pulling you down on me, bouncing on my dick."

"Fuck, Connor."

"Are you close?" I ask.

"So close."

"I know. I can see it. You want it, need it, don't you?"

"So bad," he breathes.

"Come for me," I whisper, watching as he does, long streams of cum landing on his stomach.

"Shit, James," I call as I follow him.

"Fuck, that's hot," he mumbles.

"It's messy as fuck," I say, leaning over to grab some tissues to clean up with.

"But oh so worth it," he retorts.

"Definitely."

CHAPTER 9

"You're in a good mood," Chloe says as I take my seat in English.

I shrug. "I'm not allowed to be in a good mood?"

"No, you are, it's just a bit suspicious given how you left here yesterday."

"I had a good night," I tell her.

"What's his name?" she asks.

"James."

"Oooh. Strong, solid, no nonsense. I like it."

"I'm so glad I have your approval."

"Isn't that the point of us being besties? We get to approve each other's choices."

I tilt my head to the side. "I don't remember anything about us being besties."

She shoves me as I laugh.

"Don't worry, no approval needed. It's purely casual. We haven't even met yet."

"You met online?" she asks.

MEGAN LOWE

"Poundr."

"You have any pics?"

"We had a mutual masturbation session over FaceTime last night, does that work?"

She shoves me again. "What if he's some creepy old dude?"

"A creepy old dude does *not* have the body I saw last night, and even if he did, I don't know that I'd mind. A body that fine could make a guy do stupid things."

"Like jerk off over FaceTime."

I shrug. "Like you've never sent nudes to someone."

"Who's sending nudes?" Thomas asks as he comes in the door. "Fontana, you sending them? 'Cause if you are, throw one my way." His eyes trail up and down her body.

"I'll throw this," she says, giving him the finger.

"Good. I like my women feisty," he says before taking his seat.

I brace myself for the acerbic wit of Cavanaugh McLaughlin.

"Fag," he hisses as he walks past. There's been the odd slur thrown here and there from Cav. Nothing that I didn't get at my old school, or when I walked down the street with whatever guy I happened to be seeing at the time back in Michigan.

I roll my eyes. "Yup, you got me."

Chloe elbows me.

As he walks past, he leans down. "Too bad for you I don't want you or your piece of shit car."

. . .

I'm playing with a carrot stick when Chloe slides onto the bench opposite me in the cafeteria. I know I shouldn't be surprised or hurt at what Cav said but... The constant hate, the animosity when I've done nothing to deserve it? It wears on you. It *is* wearing on me and I don't know how much more I can take. I thought the car would, I don't know, not bond us 'cause that's stupid, but could at least show him we have something in common, that we're not as different as we seem. That it would show him that I'm not a bad guy, I'm just a guy who can appreciate a classic piece of American muscle.

She leans over and pinches my cheeks. "Oh, cheer up, you sad sack. You can't seriously still be moping about that burn Cav gave you in English."

"I'm not."

"If you say so."

She laughs.

"Hi," a very busty brunette says as she sidles over to Chloe and me. She looks familiar, but I have no idea what her name is.

"Hi," I say back, resting my back against our lunch table.

"I'm EJ."

"EJ?" I ask.

She rolls her eyes. "EJ Caldwell. It's short for Elizabeth Jane, but I hate it and only my mom calls me that, so EJ."

"Right. So tell me, EJ, what can I do for you today?"

She grabs a lock of hair and twirls it around her finger. "Just wanted to come over and say hi."

"Like the official Windswept Academy welcoming committee?" I ask.

She nods. "Something like that."

"Just a month late."

She blushes. "I was working up the courage to come talk to you."

"Am I that scary that it took so long?"

She tilts her head; an attempt to look coy, I'm sure.

"Scary? No. But intimidatingly hot? Yeah."

"Intimidatingly hot?"

She nods.

"So, what can I do for you today, EJ?" I ask.

She sits on my lap and starts playing with the hair at the nape of my neck.

"Ah…." I try to move away from her, but it's a bit difficult as I'm trapped by the table behind me and EJ in front of me.

"Tell me, Connor," she all but purrs, "are you single?"

I chuckle and rub my chin. "Um, yeah, I am but—"

"Well, isn't that the best news I've heard all day?"

I look over to Chloe, struggling to hide her laugh. I shoot her a look, but she shakes her head and covers her mouth.

In desperation, I look around the cafeteria and find Cav's eyes, piercing blue-gray, seemingly staring right into my soul. I want to say that I'm able to ignore it, that it doesn't get my insides humming, or better yet, that it turns me right off, but that would be a lie—despite all the warnings and the look he's giving me. If looks could kill, I'd be ten feet under right now. But why? Is he interested in EJ? Or is he mad that for once there's some attention on someone other than him?

"So do you?" EJ asks, breaking my reverie.

"Huh?"

"I asked if you liked to party," she says.

"Oh, um, I guess?"

She laughs and plays with the top button of my shirt. "That's funny."

"How's that?" I ask.

She shrugs. "I don't know, it just is."

I nod. "Right."

"Now, Connor, you've been here a month," she says. "How come an absolute hunk like yourself doesn't have a girlfriend? Or have you not found the right girl?" She presses her boobs into my chest.

I gently grab her and shift her off my lap. "I'm gay," I tell her.

She jumps. "Oh."

I give her my winning smile. "Sorry."

"So you're really not into girls?" EJ asks.

I shake my head. "Afraid not, darlin'."

Her shoulders drop. "Are you're sure?"

"I'm very sure, but I'm flattered by the attention and for the offer." I grab her hand and press a kiss to her palm. As I do, I look up and see Cav still watching me, eyes narrowed, arms folded across his chest.

I reach up and brush her hair away from her ear. "But if I ever change my mind, I know who to come to."

She giggles and blushes.

A crash comes from the other side of the cafeteria, and I look up in time to see Cav storming away from his table.

"What's his problem?" Chloe asks.

I shrug. "I have no idea." But despite all my vows and pledges to stay away from him, I'm dying to find out.

CHAPTER 10

As usual, Jase is waiting for me once the school day is over.

I sling an arm around him as we walk toward the car. I still can't believe Amy got me a car, let alone an R-SPEC. She did really well and I know I probably didn't deserve the generosity. But that doesn't mean I'm going to tell her that.

Cars were Mom and my thing. She loved them as much, if not *more* than I do. I know if she were still alive that we'd probably scour the classifieds for a vintage one and spend every waking hour on fixing it up. She was never afraid to have grease under her nails, or oil smudged on her face. But she would've loved this car too.

When we get closer to it, there's a large crowd no doubt admiring the beauty that is my 'Stang.

"Ah, Con...," Jase says.

"Mmm?"

"Look." He nods to the side of my car. There's a massive scratch down the side, and the car is riding low.

The back window has been smashed, and the side mirrors are dangling along the sides of the car.

"The fuck?" I rush to it, running my fingers along the damage. "Someone's smashed it and keyed it."

"Slashed the tires too," Jase adds, nodding.

Cav sidles up and peers around my car. "Oof," he says, shaking his head. "You really should be more careful. Such horrible damage on such a pretty car."

"You son of a bitch." Jase holds me back as I rush Cav.

He laughs. "Guess it doesn't even look good now."

"Did you do this?" I ask. My eyes are blurred with the tears I'm trying to hold back.

He shrugs.

"Seriously?" I screech. "What the fuck, man? What have I done to you? I'm just a normal person, an ordinary student, trying to get through this year."

"You're in my way," he says.

"In your way?" I ask. "In your way of what?"

He leans closer to me. "I don't like you. I don't like your shiny, plastic car, I don't like your smug smile, I don't like you shoving your sexuality in my face."

"My what? How am I shoving that in your face?" I'm so confused right now. I thought I was doing a good job in not making waves, but apparently I was dead wrong.

"Take this as a lesson," he says, before getting in his car and driving off

"What was that about?" Chloe asks.

"I have no idea. He's like… unhinged or something."

She pats me on the shoulder. "Still find him hot and interesting?"

"Yes, but no, but what the hell?" I run a hand through my hair.

"I told you, he's not someone you want to get involved with."

"But I'm not involved with him." As much as I might fantasize about it.

"You want to be though, don't you?"

"I just...." I trail off. I don't know. I haven't done anything to Cav. Sure, I've got a crush on him, but that's it. It's not something I would ever act on. And it's not like he would go for me either. So why the animosity? Why is he coming after me? "I didn't do anything," I whisper.

"And he's making sure it stays that way," Chloe says. She reaches up to kiss me on the cheek. "Just leave him alone."

"Whatever," I grumble. "I guess I have to call a tow to get this thing home."

She gives my arm a squeeze before she walks away.

"Dude...," Jase says once we're alone.

"I know," I tell him.

"Amy is going to flip when she sees this."

"I know, but there's not a whole lot I can do about it, is there?"

"Why'd he do it?"

"Because he's a psycho. I don't know, Jase. The guy is not normal. He's egotistical and maniacal and untouchable, and—"

"Oh, come *on*," Jase says.

"What?"

"You *still* like him? Even after he did this?"

"Wha...? No! How did you get that?" I ask.

71

He shakes his head. "Your eyes went all glassy and you got this dreamy look on your face. I've gotta say, that even for you, this is a new low."

I shake my head. "I'm trying not to cry, you idiot."

"Uh-huh, *sure*."

"I don't like Cav, Jase."

"It's okay if you do, I hear hate sex is totally a thing."

"Hate sex? What the...? How the fuck do you know about that?"

"I'm fifteen, not five," he reminds me. "Guys say all sorts of shit when they're trying to impress other guys."

"You should *not* know about anything like that."

"Whatever. You can't keep me in the dark my whole life, and don't think I'm going to forget about how you *still* like Cavanaugh McLaughlin."

I sigh and run a hand through my hair. "I'm fucked, aren't I?"

He smiles. "On several different levels."

Predictably, when Amy gets home and sees my car, she's livid.

"You've had it *four* days," she shrieks. "*Four* days."

"I can't be responsible for what dickheads at school do. It's not like *I* did this. But it's still in one piece, and I'll get the damage fixed. Out of my own pocket," I add before she can ask.

"Okay, good." Her shoulders drop. "Just please tell me you didn't do anything to deserve this."

I put my hands on her shoulders. "It's just a small personality clash. I'm sure it'll work itself out soon."

"Are you sure? I can go to the school if you're having difficulties."

"It'll be fine, I promise." I take a breath. I can't deny Amy's trying. I guess I should too. If not for her sake, then for Jase's. So I will. "And I'm sorry, for everything. I was hurting and—"

I'm cut off when she throws her arms around me. "I'm sorry too," she whispers.

We're rocked when Jase wraps his arms around us as well.

"This is like some *Brady Bunch* shit," he says as we break apart.

"Don't swear," Amy scolds.

He shrugs. "It's nice to finally see you two get your sh —act together," he corrects.

"If I'd known all it would take was a car, I would've got you one earlier," Amy says, wiping her eyes.

"Mom always said I was born with gasoline in my veins."

Her eyes go soft. "She did."

"So when can I get a car?" Jase asks. "'Cause I've been looking, and I think I'd like a—"

"Just a minute there, mister," Amy says. "First of all, you need to wait until you can get your permit. Then when you've done all that and you get your license, we can *talk* about getting you a car and what kind it is. But, as that day is a while off, you're going to have to hold your horses and be content with Connor and me driving you around."

"But you'll let me borrow your car when the time comes, right, Con?"

I throw my head back and laugh. "Yeah, not a chance in hell. But good try."

His shoulders slump. "You guys suck."

I look to Amy, and we both shrug.

"Ugh!" he cries, throwing his arms up.

"About the car—" Amy starts.

I hold up a hand. "I'll get it fixed. I've already got a call in to a few places."

She nods. "I appreciate that, but that's not what I was going to say. I was going to say that I acknowledge it wasn't your fault, and I'm glad you're being proactive to fix it. But if this 'clash' with this kid gets any worse, I want you to know that I'm serious in my offer to go to the school." She swallows. "Mom and Dad left us more than enough for good futures, I'm sure they wouldn't mind if I threw some of it around. In fact, it might be fun."

I bring her in and kiss the top of her head. "Thanks, Aims."

She looks up at me. "I really did mean it when I said I'm sorry." Tears well in her eyes.

"I know. I did too."

"But you're still not getting a car," she says to Jase.

"You guys suck," he replies, going off to sulk in his room.

Later that night, I lie on my bed, staring at the ceiling, thinking about everything that happened today.

Connor: Hey, you around?

All I want is to hear a friendly voice, see a friendly

face, and maybe, just maybe, we can have another mutual masturbation session. I mean, it would make me feel a *little* bit better about what went down today.

Connor: James? You there?

I know I'm treading into dangerous territory here with my feelings, but I can't help it. He's a great guy who I have incredible chemistry with, something that's not so easy to find. And he listens to me. That might sound strange, considering we've never met, but you can read or hear words but not hear what the person who's saying them means. James does. And sure, right now the timing may not be right, but maybe once this year is over and he can get a little distance, things might be different. A guy can hope, at least.

Connor: I guess you're busy, which is cool. I just had a shitty day today, and at the risk of sounding sappy, I wanted to hear your voice.

Connor: Anyway, I hope you had a good day and if you didn't then I'm here if you want to talk about it.

Connor: Or not talk about it.

Connor: Whatever works for you.

Connor: Okay, I'm gonna stop now before I make an even bigger idiot of myself.

Connor: But have a good night.

CHAPTER 11

In the end, Amy and I went halves on the damage to my car. I told her she didn't have to, but she said as a reward for my continued good behavior, she'd pay half.

So while things between Amy and me are good, it appears my relationship with James has cooled significantly, and by cooled, I mean he's ghosted me. I have his profile picture up, that stupid star-shaped scar haunting me.

"I know you're into some strange stuff," Jase says as he sits down next to me, "but staring at a picture of a hand is just fucking weird."

I cuff him over the back of his head. "Watch your mouth. If Amy hears you swearing, she'll blame me and take my car off me, and neither of us wants that."

He mimes zipping his lips. "But seriously, who's the dude?"

I close the picture. "Just some guy I was talking to."

"Was?"

I shrug. "He ghosted. No big deal."

"Really? 'Cause your face says different."

"It's fine. He was honest with me and said he didn't have time for a relationship. I'm the idiot who didn't listen."

"You like this guy?" he asks.

I shrug again. "We had some good times. I thought we had a connection, but obviously I was wrong."

"Maybe he's just scared."

I give my brother a smile. Throughout Mom and Dad's illnesses, Jase was always there trying to make sure I had a smile on my face, always reassuring me things were going to be okay and I wasn't fucking them up. "Yeah, maybe."

"If that guy doesn't want you, then fu—stuff him. You're almost as awesome as I am, and anyone who doesn't see that is missing out *big* time."

I chuckle.

"But seriously, if he doesn't see how great you are, then you're better off without him. You don't need someone who doesn't appreciate you."

"See, this is why we keep you around," I tell him.

"Pfft, you know life would be boring AF without me."

"Did you actually say 'AF'?"

"Did you not, like, a minute ago tell me I couldn't swear otherwise Amy would take your car away? So this is what you get."

"I suppose I did bring this on myself."

"Yes, you did."

"Then I apologize."

He nods and places a hand on his chest. "Thank you. I appreciate it."

"So how's school going?" I ask.

He shrugs. "It's school."

"You making friends?"

"A couple. None as nice as yours though."

I roll my eyes.

"What's up with that, anyway?"

"What's up with what?"

"That girl the other day."

"You saw that?" I laugh. "She was the official Windswept welcoming committee." I roll my eyes.

"Seriously? How come *I* didn't get a welcome like that?"

I slap him over the head. "You're a freshman, put it back in your pants."

It's his turn to laugh.

"But seriously, she was just a girl who wanted to get on all the goodness that is Connor Siddell."

"Barf. Doesn't she know you're gay?" he asks.

"It didn't seem to matter to her."

"Huh."

I run a hand over my chest. "I mean, I *am* a fine specimen of a male. Who wouldn't want me?"

Jase throws a cushion at me as I laugh. "But seriously, kid, I'm always going to want to make sure you're okay, so if you're not fitting in or you're having issues with someone—"

"You'll what?" he asks.

"I'd do my best to help you."

He sighs and slumps on the cushions beside me. "That's the thing, Con, you can't help me with everything, no matter how much you want to. Some things have to come from me."

"I know, but old habits die hard."

"I miss them, you know. A lot."

I sling an arm around his shoulders and pull him to my side. "I do too."

"Do you think this is really what they'd want for us? To move away from our friends and everything we know, to come here?"

"I think they'd want us to be with Amy, and she has a life here. It makes sense for us to come here, seeing as she's supporting us." Don't get me started on how weird it is to be the one defending Amy now. But it would do neither of us any good by saying I think we should've stayed in Michigan. Besides, Amy and I are in a good place right now.

"Why is life so easy for you?" he asks me.

"What's easy?"

"Everything. Making friends, school, looking after me, moving on from Mom and Dad."

"Hey." I move so I can look him in the eyes. "None of that *is* easy for me. Yes, I have a good friend in Chloe, and we have fun, but that was luck. School isn't easy. Look at what Cav did to my car. But the rest? Buddy, I will *never* move on from Mom and Dad's deaths. *Never*. But I know there's nothing I can do to bring them back. With the amount of pain they were in at the end, I don't know, I kind of... wished it could be over, for their sakes. Don't get me wrong, I didn't want them to go, but I wanted the pain to end, and there was only one way that was going to happen. Maybe I should've shown you that, but I didn't want that to be your last memory of them.

"And as for looking after you? Why wouldn't I? You

were all I had left, all I could count on, the one who was keeping me sane, helping to keep my shit together. That was never a job for me. It never will be."

He sighs. "It's just hard."

I sit back on the couch. "I know. We all have our bad days, but we've got to remember that we've got each other and it'll be okay."

"What are you going to do about the guy?" he asks.

I sigh and run a hand through my hair. "Not much I *can* do about him. If he doesn't want to talk to me, there's not much I can do about it. Clearly it's his loss, but whatever."

"You like him."

"Yeah, I do, or did, I guess. He did say we would never be a thing but...."

"But you were hoping he'd change his mind."

"Yeah, or something."

"And all this stuff with Cav?"

I blow out a breath. "I don't know. I want, *so* badly, to bring him down a peg or two, but I don't know if that won't just cause more trouble for me."

He nods. "Yeah, probably."

"But I don't think it's right he gets away with everything."

"It's not, but he's like, the king of Windswept, you don't want to go against that."

"Yeah, I know...."

"But you've still got your girly crush. I get it, the guy is very pretty."

I give him a playful shove. "That doesn't excuse all manner of sins," I tell him.

"But if he was open to it?"

"In Jase's dream world where everything is unicorns and rainbows and Cavanaugh McLaughlin didn't have a chip the size of the Bean on his shoulder and wasn't a homophobic bastard, then sure, I'd give him a go. But this is the real world and Cav *does* have that chip on his shoulder and *is* a homophobic bastard."

"What is it that fascinates you about him so much?"

"I don't know. Maybe it's the fact that he's so closed off or acts so tough, when you know no *one* can be that tough without a weakness. Or the fact that he thinks his car is God's gift to racers, or that he thinks *he* is God's gift." I shrug. "There's just something about him." That, and I'm *certain* there's something he's hiding, something he doesn't want people to know about. He's too controlled, too packaged, too perfect. There's something there, and I want to be the one who finds it. Despite his best efforts, Cavanaugh McLaughlin is getting under my skin.

CHAPTER 12

Pulling into school the next day, I forgo the space I previously occupied, opting for one in the middle row, in between a BMW and a Mercedes.

Jase chuckles. "I'm pretty sure if someone wanted to get to your car, they'd still be able to find it here."

"Maybe I'm trying to be more humble and not flash around my goods."

This time he actually snorts. "Uh-huh, *sure*."

By this stage Chloe has walked up.

"Why are you parking all the way back here?" she asks.

"He's hiding," Jase answers as we both get out.

"I am not," I argue.

"Sure looks like it."

"Can we just leave it?" I ask. "It's a fucking parking space; it doesn't mean shit." I start walking toward the school building as Cav pulls in, slowing down as he drives past me, not breaking eye contact until he absolutely has to.

"Shit, that was hot," Chloe says, coming up beside me.

"Huh?"

"You, Cav, that little standoff you guys just had." The "duh" is implied.

"He's just trying to intimidate me," I say.

"Probably. And at risk of getting you all hot and bothered, I think you're getting to him."

"I don't want to get to him."

"Really?"

"Of course I don't. You saw what he did to my car."

"That is true. Why did he do that, again?"

"Because he's a psycho, like you've been telling me all along."

"Hmm, yeah, that sounds about right."

"But seriously," I say as I stop. "What is with that guy? I've done nothing to him and he attacks my car? Like, what the fuck? I don't even care how good-looking he is, he's insane."

"You don't care... Oh my God," she says. "You seriously like him."

"What?" I ask, my cheeks flushing.

"You, Connor Siddell, like Cavanaugh McLaughlin. I thought it was one of those silly little girl crushes, but you seriously like him. You want him."

"Be real," I tell her.

"Oh, I *am*."

"I do not like Cavanaugh McLaughlin. He's an ass."

"He has a *fine* ass," she corrects. "Bet it would be nice and tight for you to push into."

"Stop it," I tell her, trying my hardest not to imagine doing the very thing she described.

"You're imagining it, aren't you? How tight, how firm,

how muscular he'd be. How he'd be able to manhandle you and fight to show you who's boss."

I try, unsuccessfully, to subtly adjust myself to hide my semi.

Chloe chuckles. "Yeah, you're not thinking about it at all. But seriously," she says as we watch Thomas greet Cav, "do we need to talk about this?"

"No." I sigh. "It's stupid, I know this. I guess it's just been a while since I've had some action that wasn't by my own hand. I hear deprivation can make you crazy."

She rolls her eyes. "There's always EJ if you're desperate."

I shove her gently. "I'm sure she's more your type than she is mine."

She grimaces. "I mean, she's hot but she's also a total space cadet. I'm not even sure *if* I went for her, she'd understand what was happening."

I laugh and sling an arm around her shoulders. "Looks like we're both shit out of luck then, aren't we?"

I know Cav is watching us as we walk into the building, but this is enough for now.

Chloe isn't in English. She's been called to the guidance counselor, so she texts me to let me know and ask if I can take notes for her. Given this, it's a surprise when someone slides into her seat. His scent, rich, woodsy with a hint of engine oil, surrounds me.

"What's the deal with you and Caldwell?" he asks.

I lean back and turn to face him. "What's it to you?" I hit back.

"Just wondering how it works, that's all."

"Ah, I see, you need tips on how to get the hot girls." The words are out of my mouth before I realize what I've said. But it's not like this hasn't been a long time coming. Cav's here and I want answers.

"Ha! If, and that's a big fucking if, I did need tips, why the fuck would I come to you?"

"You mean the resident gay guy?" I ask, putting it front and center. *He* may have a problem with my sexuality, but I sure as shit don't.

"Is it a ploy? For either you or Fontana to plow Caldwell? Is that it? You're pretending to be straight, then one night she has one too many drinks, you get her where you want her, and then you and Fontana swap, is that it? A bait and switch."

I clench my fists. "Don't confuse me with one of your goons," I tell him. "That may be how they get girls in bed, but it's definitely not the way Chloe goes about things."

"My goons?" he asks. "What do they have to do with this?"

"I'm sure more than one of them has tried, unsuccessfully, to get into Chloe's pants. Probably EJ's as well."

"So you're hoping the guys will be ripe for the picking after the girls reject them, is that it?"

"First off, I don't know what EJ wants. She came up to me yesterday, we had a chat, and then we went our separate ways. If Chloe is interested in her, I'm sure she can get her without my help. I don't need any help either. I might be gay but that doesn't make me some sexual predator, poised to take advantage of every guy Chloe rejects. But it would be nice if you could tell your *friends* that she's not some object to be obtained or a game to be played."

"I don't tell my friends shit."

"I know, it shows."

He growls, literally growls at me.

I shake my head. "For fuck's sake, man, have some balls. You know what your reputation is here. How about for once, just for once, you use it to do some good? But then, that would require being a decent human being, wouldn't it? I guess it's a good thing she's got balls of her own and doesn't need you or anyone."

"She doesn't need balls, although maybe they'd come in handy when she's trying to seduce all the straight girls around here. Maybe you'd like them too."

I laugh. "If Chloe had balls, I would indeed like her better. At least that's something you got right."

"You need to stay away from me," he chokes out.

"I wasn't the one who sat down next to me. That was all you. Since the first day I got here I've been wanting to keep a low profile. I'm just here with my friend and that's it. I haven't done anything to you, haven't said anything to you, I've just been me."

"I told you, you're in my way."

"And I've told you I don't know what way I'm in, but it definitely isn't yours. *You're* the one who keeps coming back, who keeps coming after me. Why is that?"

He pushes his chair back with a screech.

I shake my head. "You say this, whatever *this* is, is all me? I think it's all *you*. *You're* the one with the problem, not me."

He clenches his jaw and fists as he stands up. "Don't talk to me."

I throw my hands up. "I didn't do anything. I *never* do anything. *You're* the one who sat down here. I was just minding my own business."

He shoves the chair out of his way as he walks past.

While I can't say these... interactions with Cav are entirely pleasant, I also can't deny that I'm growing to like them. There something with Cav, something that keeps him coming back at me. And I'm determined to find out what it is.

CHAPTER 13

"I heard you and Cav got into it in English this morning," Chloe says as she sits down at our table in the cafeteria. "I thought I told you not to do that if I wasn't there?"

"What was I supposed to do? Tell him, sorry, we can't do this right now, Chloe isn't here?"

"Uh, yeah."

I shake my head.

"I heard it got pretty heated."

I take a bite of my salad. "He said some things; I said some things."

"About what?" she asks.

"You, EJ," I roll my eyes. "Honestly, I have no idea."

She shakes her head. "What the fuck is going on with you two?"

"I have no idea! From the start I've tried to keep a low profile but he won't let me."

"*He* won't let you?"

"I know, it sounds stupid, but what other explanation

is there? You know I don't do anything that would upset him—"

"Except fantasize about his dreamy eyes." She puts her hands under her chin and flits her eyelashes at me.

I push her face away, laughing.

"And I know I shouldn't have taken the bait today, but after what he did to my car…. I don't know, I'd just… had enough of all his shit."

She nods.

"But that was the first time I've outwardly stood up to him."

She pats my hand. "I get it. And I wish I could tell you why Cav has picked you as his victim but well, I really don't think we want to delve into his mind. Who knows what we might find."

I laugh. "Thanks, Chlo."

"But I would recommend you find another reason to flirt with him."

"I was not flirting with him."

She raises an eyebrow. "And I'm not gay."

"I *don't* like Cavanaugh McLaughlin."

"You do, but that's okay. Even I can appreciate the 'falling for the bad boy' thing. I'd say I have the 'falling for the bad girl' thing, but, well, I *am* the bad girl. How's your little Poundr buddy by the way?"

"He, uh, stopped responding to my texts the other day."

"That's gotta suck."

I shrug. "It is what it is. He told me when we first started talking that he wouldn't have a lot of time once school started, I guess I just thought…."

"That he'd find time for you."

I nod. "Yeah. I know it sounds stupid. I mean, don't we all think we're going to be the one to change a person?"

"We do, but I kinda like that deep down we're all kind of optimists."

I smile and give her a nudge. "Doesn't mean it doesn't hurt any less when it inevitably fails to happen."

"No, it doesn't, but hope is a good thing. Except when it comes to Cavanaugh McLaughlin."

I groan. "For the last time, yes, I like him, but no, I'm not going to do anything about it. He's a crush, nothing more, nothing less. It'll be like that time when I had a crush on Scott Eastwood when he starred in *The Longest Ride*." I swoon for a bit, remembering him on that bull.

Chloe clicks her fingers in front of my face.

"Sorry."

She rolls her eyes.

"You're hopeless."

"Didn't we establish early on in this relationship I was the romantic one?"

"Yeah, but do you have to be so... soppy?"

"Soppy? How am I soppy?"

"I don't know. Your eyes got all cloudy and I could tell you were imagining you and him on a beach somewhere, all loved up."

I give her a shove. "It was a farm by the way."

She laughs. "Still, I want you to stay away from Cav."

"I do! Honestly, I don't know what more I can do, short of transferring to a new school and that won't happen."

"Are you sure that's not an option?"

"Yup."

She sighs.

"Look, I'm sure it'll be okay. I'll just keep doing what I'm doing, or not doing as the case may be, and I'm sure he'll get bored with me sooner or later."

She scoffs. "If you say so."

I nod. "I do." The truth is, I don't, but what else can I do?

"Want to put a bet on it?"

CHAPTER 14

I'm walking with Jase that afternoon after school when I'm shoved from behind and into the side of my car.

"What the…?" I spin around and come face-to-face with Cav. "What the fuck is your problem?" I ask.

"Are you betting on me?" he yells.

"The fuck?" I ask.

"I heard you were betting on me. I don't want any part of your sick games."

"*My* sick games? I'm not playing any games. I'm just trying to go to school, learn some shit, and not cause any trouble. You're the one who has a problem with me, and who vandalized my car."

He crosses his arms over his chest. "You should be more careful where you park. Accidents happen all the time."

"Message received," I say, gesturing to our current location.

"Good. I don't want your fairy germs anywhere near my car. Who knows what diseases you carry."

"That's right," I say. "Car-to-car transmission is a common way to contract illnesses."

"Who knows what diseases you sickos have. They could be transmitted any way."

"That's true," I tell him. "I mean, we secretly make up traps to entice normal, straight people to go gay, so why shouldn't we add biological warfare to our arsenal?"

He nods. "That's right."

I roll my eyes. "Whatever you say."

"You can't turn me gay, either."

"Who said I was trying?"

"I want you to stop this bet."

"Just out of curiosity," I say as I lean against my car. "How did you hear about this so-called 'bet'?"

"One of the guys told me, said they heard it at lunch."

I nod. "And that makes it legit, does it?"

"I know you," he tells me. "I know what you and your... *type* are like."

"Ah, yes, the 'preying on the innocent' stereotype, one of my personal favorites." I sigh. "Look, I don't know how many times I can tell you that I don't want any trouble, but I sincerely mean it."

"I want you to leave me out of your games."

I hold my hands up. "There are no games, but whatever."

"I don't believe you," he grits out.

"Fine, don't believe me, that's totally up to you."

I turn away from him and unlock my car. Jase yells out as my head is slammed against the roof of the car, my eyes level with Cav's hand. A hand with a unique star-shaped scar on it.

"James?" I whisper.

"What?"

The pressure on my head and back disappears.

I turn around and face him. "Show me your hand," I demand, my head starting to pound, but that scar, *James's* scar is enough for me to ignore it for the time being. Suddenly, it all makes sense. Why he was so angry at me. Why he kept coming at me. Because I know his secret.

"The fuck? No."

"Afraid I might see your scar and figure out who you are?" I ask. "It's too late, I already saw it; I already *know* who you are."

"You don't know shit."

"Oh, but I do," I say, taking a step closer to him. James is *here*. The guy I've been falling for, the one I've poured my heart out to, the one who *listened* while I did, is here. "How many hours have we spent on the phone? How many texts have we sent? I know what gets you hard, I've *seen* you get off."

I crowd him against the car neighboring mine.

"Why did you ghost me?" I ask.

He pushes me back. "You don't know what you're talking about."

"No?"

"No," he confirms.

I go to pull out my phone. "Would you like me to show you? I haven't deleted a thing. I've kept it all, rereading it, watching the clips you sent me over and over and over. They get me hard. Every. Single. Time." I feel like all my Christmases have come at once. James, here, in front of me.

He smacks the phone out of my hand. "You don't know what you're talking about."

"I'm talking about you being gay. I'm talking about the relationship we were building. I'm talking about how I know you, the *real* you."

He grabs me by the throat, throwing me against my car again.

"I'm *not* him," he grits out.

"Not here," I manage to squeeze out. "And maybe not even at home, but you can be with me."

He squeezes my throat once more before shoving me away. "I don't know who the fuck you think you are, who you think *I* am, but you're dead fucking wrong. If you think you can play with me, it won't fucking work. Leave me the fuck alone. You don't know shit. You don't know shit," he repeats, his chest heaving.

I put my hands up. "Okay. It's okay. We're all good here," I tell him.

He shakes his head. "Don't. Don't give me that pitying look. I don't need it, and I sure as fuck don't want it."

"Absolutely no pity here."

He points at me. "I know your type. You're going to try to get in my head, make me think things that aren't real, or make me do things I don't want to do. It's not going to work. It's not going to work!"

"All right, all right," Thomas says, pulling Cav back by the shoulders. Obviously our arguing alerted the guard dog. "Let's not bring more attention to this than we need to, huh?"

"Get off me," Cav says as he struggles in Thomas's hold.

"Are you gonna be cool?" he asks.

"I'm fine, it's this pedo we need to worry about."

I'm more worried about Cav's rapid mood swing than I am about responding to the slur he leveled at me.

Thomas looks to me, and I hold my hands up. "I didn't do anything, I swear."

He nods and drags Cav a few feet away. "Come on, man, let's go to Giordano's and get some deep dish, huh?"

I don't know whether it was the lure of pizza or if the fight had gone out of him, but he allows Thomas to pull him along and into his car.

"What the hell was that about?" Jase asks.

"I honestly don't know," I reply.

"Did you call him James?"

"I thought I saw something, a scar."

"Like the one on the hand of the guy you were talking to?"

"Yeah, like that. But I must have been seeing things." There's no way Cav is James, that James is Cav. He can't be. James is... everything that Cav isn't. They're complete opposites in every way. But yet.... I did say I think Cav is hiding something, and this is *definitely* something.

"Why? Because the hand belongs to Cavanaugh McLaughlin?"

I whirl to face him. "Promise me you won't say anything about this to anyone," I say.

He nods. "I promise."

"I'm serious, Jase, you can't say anything, don't even hint at it, nothing. Not even to Chloe okay?"

"I get it. I won't say anything."

"Good. Thank you."

"But why, though? I thought you liked him."

"I do—or I did, whatever. But people can't know, okay?" I don't know why I want to keep this to myself—or myself and Jase, I guess. It would be karma and then some if I were to spill the tea on Cav, but something is stopping me. The part of him that might be James is stopping me. James doesn't deserve this. And if there's even a *slight* chance that Cav *could* be James? Then I want to protect that, to see if I can't get it back, to see if I can't have it all the time.

"Why are you protecting him? The things he said…. They were pretty horrible."

I run a hand through my hair. "I just am, okay? Can we drop it?"

"Yeah, that's fine."

"Good." I bend down and pick up my phone, relieved that somehow it isn't smashed to bits.

"I know I said I'd drop it," Jase says when we get in the car, "but I have one more question."

I blow out a breath. "What is it, bud?"

"What the heck are you going to do now?"

CHAPTER 15

Connor: Why didn't you tell me?

Connor: You know this doesn't change anything between us if you don't want it to.

Connor: But how great is it that we found each other?

Connor: None of the stuff that happened at school matters, okay?

Connor: I don't even care if we keep things how they were. Enemies at school, but together out of it.

Connor: I'm sorry for being such a douchebag though. I thought there was something more, something behind your façade.

Connor: I want to get to know you, the real you, the mix between Cav and James.

Connor: We could be great, you know.

I'm typing out my ninth message when I finally get one back, telling me the number has been disconnected.

I flick to Poundr and the message thread we had there, but his account's been deleted.

I sigh, dropping my phone on my chest before folding my hands behind my head, staring at the roof.

Cavanaugh McLaughlin is James.

James is Cavanaugh McLaughlin.

On one hand, I'm ecstatic. He's here, he's *so* close. But on the other? What am I supposed to do now? I want to be with him but how?

"Hey," Amy says, knocking on my door.

"What's up?" I ask.

"Just making sure you're okay. Jase said some stuff happened at school today?"

"Stupid boy stuff. Nothing to worry about."

"Do we, um, need to have the talk or set some, um, ground rules?"

I smile. "Mom and Dad had the talk with me when I was twelve. They had it with Jase too. As for ground rules? It's your house."

"It's *our* house," she corrects.

"But you're like, the parental figure, so I guess if you think we need to set rules, then set them up."

"Will you follow them?"

"As long as they're not ridiculous, I will."

"What's ridiculous?"

"Hmm." I think about it. "Stuff like being in bed by eight, eating all my vegetables, getting straight A's."

She nods. "How about this? School night curfew is ten thirty, 1:00 a.m. on Fridays and Saturdays. I promise not to feed you veggies you hate, but I expect you to eat the ones you don't. As for schoolwork? I'd love it if you could get all A's, but as long as you're maintain at least a C+ average, we won't have a problem. Deal?"

I nod. "Deal."

"As for having boys over—"

"It's not like I can get them pregnant," I remind her.

"No, but STDs can stay with you longer than a kid," she points out. "Just be careful. You're over the age of consent, but make sure anyone you're with is as well."

"Got it."

"Is there, um, anything you want to ask of me?" she says, looking down at the floor.

"Really?" I ask.

She shrugs. "You're eighteen now, legally an adult. It's time I treat you like one, don't you think?"

"Ah, yeah?"

She chuckles. "I'm trying here. I'm not Mom and Dad, and after everything you went through with them, you had to grow up fast. I can't try to dictate how you act; I don't have any right to. So, I figure we're more like… roommates. We both have our own lives and are free to do whatever we want, within reason. Given this, it's only fair you ask things of me too."

"Um, when you put it that way…."

She nods.

"I guess if you want to have someone over, clothes are to be worn in all the common areas."

She smiles. "Agreed."

"And he's not to play the father role. To me *or* Jase. Even if I'm at college or whatever, that'll never be anyone's role."

"Also agreed."

"And no dissing the Lions in my presence. They are my team; we are one pride."

She rolls her eyes, but nods anyway. "Fair enough. But you have to realize this is Chicago, Bears territory. You are going to get shit, especially for supporting Detroit."

"Can we compromise, and I'll support the Cubs?" I ask.

She narrows her eyes. "Is that because of Kris Bryant?"

I sigh. "The man is too beautiful for words."

She laughs. "Yes, yes, he is. So, is that it?"

I nod. "I think so."

"And you're okay with this boy stuff you've got going on?"

"Not really, but I will be."

"You know you can talk to me if you want to. I-I know I haven't been there before when you needed me, and that's completely on me, but I'm here now, and I want to help."

"Thanks, Aims."

"I really am sorry. For not being there, for not helping you and Jase…."

She sniffs. I get off the bed and fold her into my arms.

"And I'm sorry for being a bastard about it. I know you had your reasons; I should've respected that."

She shakes her head. "I should've come back."

"There wasn't much you could've done. There wasn't much any of us could."

"Still, I could've been there, with you and Jase."

"You're here now; we're here now. They-they wouldn't want us to be at each other's throats. They'd want us to help one another."

She nods.

"How about we both agree to leave all that in the past?

You made mistakes; I made mistakes. It was a shitty time for everyone."

"Okay," she sniffs.

"Jase!" I yell.

"Yeah?" he says, popping his head out of his room.

"Get your ass over here, we're having a family hug."

"Er, okay." He lopes over and puts his arms around us. "Can I ask what this is about?"

"Amy and I were just discussing how we're not gonna let you out until you're thirty. Won't be able to get a car until you're fifty."

"Aww, c'mon guys, that's fucked-up."

"Hey!" Amy says.

"It is!" Jase insists. "Just 'cause I'm the youngest doesn't mean you can baby me for the rest of my life."

I pinch his cheeks. "But you were such a cute baby."

He smacks my hand away. "Fuck off."

"Hey!" Amy says again. "We may not baby you for the rest of your life, but at fifteen you're not too old to be grounded."

"He started it," Jase grumbles.

"And I'm finishing it," she says, folding her arms across her chest.

"Whatever."

I look to Amy, and we both laugh.

"Come on, bud," I say, ruffling his hair. "We were just messing with you."

He knocks my hand away again.

Amy puts her arm around his shoulder. "Don't be like that, J. I got hot dogs today, and we can make come chili and do—"

"Coney Island hot dogs," he finishes for her.

"We may not be in Michigan, but we can bring Michigan to us," she says.

"Sounds good to me." And it does. I might have boy troubles right now, but I have my family, and that'll do.

CHAPTER 16

I did a lot of thinking overnight and concluded that I'm not going to let James, I mean Cav, slip through my fingers again. We had a connection. We *have* a connection. You don't find that every day.

It makes total sense why Cav is the way he is now. I know it must be hell on him trying to juggle the two sides of himself. But I can help with that. I *want* to help with that. I want to be the one he comes to when things are too much for him to handle. I want to be the one who comforts him, who makes him laugh, who makes him moan. Cavanaugh McLaughlin has wormed his way inside my heart, and I don't want to let him go. I won't let him go, not without a fight.

"You okay?" Jase asks after I park and turn the car off.

"Why wouldn't I be?" I give him my best blinding-smile-to-cover-the-fact-I'm-dying-a-little-inside smile.

He points to my face. "*That's* why."

My shoulders drop. "I think I'm doing the best I can, and I guess that's going to have to do."

He nods. "What hurts more?" he asks. "The fact he didn't tell you who he really is? The fact he's an absolute ass to you here? Or the fact that through it all, he doesn't want to be with you?"

Trust Jase to get to the heart of the matter.

I clutch my chest. "Damn, kid, hit me where it hurts, why don't ya?"

"Sorry, I just thought we'd get all that other stuff out of the way and get to the heart of the matter."

I nod, thinking about his question. "I think what hurts the most is he trusted me enough to tell me certain things about his life, and even when I expressed the desire to know more, he wouldn't let me in. I told him *everything* about us, and he couldn't even return the favor."

"Who wouldn't return the favor?" Chloe asks, resting her arm on the roof of the car and leaning in. "Is your mutual masturbation friend not being so friendly anymore?"

I chuckle. "You could say that," I reply.

She shakes her head. "I told you," she sings.

"I know, I know." I shoo her away from the car so I can get out.

"Con," Jase calls.

I turn back to face him. "I'll be okay, bud."

He gives me a look.

"I promise."

He blows out a breath and shakes his head. "Just don't do anything stupid, okay?"

"I'll try not to."

"Try not to what?" Chloe asks. "Get in another fight

with Cav? Why do you always do that when I'm not around, huh?" She threads her arm through mine and hugs it to her chest. "Tell me, Connor, why do you hate me? You always have all the fun when I'm not there." She sticks her bottom lip out and gives me puppy dog eyes.

"Given my aversion to vagina, I'd wager a *lot* of my fun is going to take place without you."

"Oh, ha ha," she deadpans.

"And I hate to break it to you, but you don't like what I've got, either."

We've just reached the front row of cars when Cav pulls in. He glares at me as he drives past. But my heart leaps at the sight of him.

Chloe laughs. "What the fuck is going on with you two?" she asks. "I know you have this weird fascination with him, no matter how many times I've tried to warn you off him, but I've never seen him actually go after someone, not like he has with you."

"Maybe he's bored?" I say.

"It doesn't seem like boredom to me."

"Maybe I hit a nerve?"

"Oh, you hit a nerve all right."

"How much do you know about him?" I ask. "I mean, *really* know about him?"

"Aside from all the usual stuff?"

"Yeah."

She sighs. "Not much. His mom's a senator, and from what I hear, she has balls, big ones. She's not one to shy away from having unpopular opinions."

"And his dad?"

"Hmm. I think he owns like, half of Chicago. Inherited it from his dad who inherited it, who inherited and blah, blah, blah. I don't think he really does much though."

"And what about this so-called 'murder' he's supposed to have committed?"

She rolls her eyes. "Honestly, I'm pretty sure that's all bravado to make him seem like a badass. A weird choice of actions if you ask me, but Cav has never been normal. But they do say death affects people in different ways."

I nod. "Were he and this guy close?"

"As close as anyone can get to Cav I guess. He, Max, and Thomas were like the three amigos. They'd known each forever, so yeah, I guess they were close, doing whatever guys do when they're friendly, you know, shaving each other's chests and braiding their back hair, I don't know."

"Why would they shave their chests and not their backs?"

She laughs. "I just said I don't know! Didn't we establish, like, first thing in this relationship that dicks aren't my thing?"

"We did, but that doesn't mean common sense goes out the window along with an X chromosome."

She pokes her tongue out.

"What exactly happened anyway? All I ever hear is that this guy died and Cav is apparently happy to take responsibility for it, never mind how fucking weird that is."

"So there was a party because there's always a party and Max just snapped. No one really knows what happened; I've heard a whole heap of things, each more unlikely than the one before it. And I guess all Cav's lackeys value their lives too much to ask him about it."

"Okay, so Max snaps. How does that lead to Cav killing him? Wouldn't it be more likely that Max tried to murder Cav? And I still don't get why he's taking responsibility for it! None of this makes sense!" I throw my hands up.

"None of us understand it, and even less of us are willing to take our lives into our own hands and actually ask about it. If he's owning responsibility for it, it's not such a great leap that he'd be willing to do something like that again."

I roll my eyes.

"Look, I've heard everything from Max was super drunk and just messing around, to Max was in love with Cav and Cav rejected him. I have no idea how anyone *knows* that, as the party was pretty much shut down when he first pulled the gun, but this is Windswept. People know all manner of things that they either can't or shouldn't know. Nothing is secret for long here."

"So Max was drunk? That seems like a reasonable motive for murder."

She hits me in the stomach. "Shut it. It's story time, so sit back and listen, will ya?"

"We're walking."

She rolls her eyes. "You know what I mean."

"Okay, continue."

"I can't remember what the party was for. I mean, we're teenagers; do we *need* an excuse to party?"

"No, we do not," I agree.

"Right. So as far as I know, and remember I'm getting all of this like, third or fourth hand, everything was fine. Nothing weird was happening, it was a normal party. The night goes on. At some stage I think Cav left. That's when Max goes nuts."

"Wait. He went nuts because Cav left, or it just coincided with him leaving?"

"I don't know, Con. He went nuts; that's all I know."

"Well, I think this might be an important fact, but if you couldn't bother to do the proper detective work…."

She rolls her eyes.

"*Anyway*, Cav is gone, and Max goes nuts. Out of nowhere, he starts ranting and raving. Obviously he'd had a lot to drink, but then, everyone had. So he's ranting and raving and then pulls out a gun."

"A gun? Where'd he get a gun?"

She shrugs. "No idea. So everyone runs inside and leaves him outside, and he's like, super agitated and not getting any better.

"Someone calls Cav. He finally shows up and goes out to talk to Max. They were talking and then they moved into the pool house, which is where absolutely no one knows what happened, except that after a while there's a gunshot, and Cav emerges, covered in blood. Max's blood."

"Was there a police investigation?" I ask.

"Of course, but this is Chicago. They said it was a suicide, but come on, it's Cavanaugh McLaughlin. Even if he *did* kill Max, they'd never say so."

"So now it's not just murder, it's a coverup?"

She shrugs. "I didn't make this up. I'm purely telling you what happened."

A hot breath comes over my neck. "Yeah, Siddell, she's just telling you what happened," Cav says. He walks around me, so he's now facing me. "So watch out, or who knows, you might be next."

CHAPTER 17

Chloe is going on about something that I'm only half listening to, staring into space instead. All this stuff with Cav and James and that Max guy is doing my head in. I can't make sense of any of it. The *only* thing I can make sense of is my feelings for James. I mean Cav. I mean… okay, maybe I can only make sense of part of it. But what I do know, is I like him. I want him. But he does not want me; at least, he doesn't want me in public. Or private seeing as though he disconnected his phone number and deleted Poundr his account, but I *know* there's something between us.

Someone hisses "fag" as he walks past. I spin around to face Cav.

"Oh," I say, rolling my eyes.

"What are you looking at?" he asks.

I hold my hands up. "Nothing. I'm not looking at anything, there's nothing to look at anyway."

"Nothing?" He quirks an eyebrow.

"That's right, nothing."

He grabs me by the front of my shirt and hauls me to my feet.

"You being cute?"

"Why would I do that?"

He shoves me away. "You know what you're doing."

"For fuck's sake!" I say, clenching my fists. "I'm not doing anything. I *never* do anything. I'm not in your way, in fact, I do my best to stay *out* of your way. Whatever problem you have with me is just that, *your* problem."

"And now you're being smart."

I nod. "Yup, that's right, I'm being smart. It's *all* about me, none of this is about *you*." I stare at the scar I know is on his hand.

Without warning he punches me. Hard. Blood drips out of my nose, and the coppery tang fills my mouth.

Everyone in the cafeteria has frozen, all eyes on us.

I laugh as I wipe the blood away. "Seriously?" I ask. Why is he doing this?

He rears back and kicks me in the stomach.

There are screams, and soft hands on me as Chloe rushes to help.

"Jesus, Connor," Chloe says. "What is wrong with you?" she asks Cav.

"Come on, man," Thomas says, grabbing Cav. "Let's get out of here." He turns to me. "Are you okay?"

I shrug, wiping at the blood coming out of my nose.

"I'll handle this," he tells me. "Why don't you go get cleaned up, huh?"

"You need to do something about him," I say. "You know I didn't do anything, that I haven't been doing anything."

"You—" Cav lunges again, but Thomas holds him back. He drags Cav away, saying stuff I can't hear.

"That was insane," Chloe says.

I laugh. "Isn't that Cav though? Isn't that what you've been telling me all this time?"

"I have, but I've never seen him do anything like this, never seen him go after anyone like he's going after you."

"Guess I should count myself lucky then."

She hauls me up and I try to ignore the amount of pain it takes to stand.

"Yeah? Feeling so lucky now?" She guides me into a bathroom.

"You know this is a girls' bathroom," I advise her as she sits me down in a waiting room thing they have in here.

"You're practically a chick. Sit your ass down," Chloe orders.

"Excuse me, I'll have you know I'm a manly man, thank you very much."

"Yeah, you're sure showing everyone just how manly you are."

"I could take him if I wanted," I say as she cleans me up.

"Am I that bad?" I ask her. "I mean, am I doing anything wrong?"

She sighs and takes a seat next to me. "Besides your little girly crush?"

I roll my eyes. "Yeah, besides that."

"Well, that probably doesn't help."

I want so badly to tell her that he, as James, was more than receptive to my attention, but I can't. I *won't*. I won't betray Cav and James's trust like that. Even though my ribs are currently screaming at me. At least the blood has stopped running out of my nose.

"I just…. I didn't want any of this. I never wanted to come to Chicago. I never wanted to come here. But now that I have to be here, I just wanted to do this year, finish high school, then get the fuck out of here. If I found a cute boy to flirt with, someone to spend some time with then that would be awesome. I know Cav isn't g-gay." I hope she doesn't notice my stutter. "But I wasn't hurting anyone with just looking at him, was I? I didn't make any moves on him, I didn't outwardly flirt with him. I just… looked."

She runs her hand over my hair. "I know. And you didn't do anything wrong, this is all Cav. For whatever reason he has something against you and I know it doesn't make sense, but he's decided there's something about you he doesn't like."

I sigh. "This is so fucked up."

She leans her head on my shoulder and I huff out a breath from the shift of weight. "Are you going to be okay?" she asks.

"Physically? I'll heal. Emotionally? Who the fuck knows."

"You know I'm here for you, right?"

I try and sling an arm around her to hug her. Eventually, with her help, I manage it. "Thank you."

"So, still got that girly crush?"

My laugh turns into a groan. "I mean, what guy can resist someone who beats him up for no reason?"

"Exactly!" she says. "Remember that when those

dreamy blue-gray eyes are peering straight into your soul—"

"I thought you were trying to help?" I ask. I know this should signal the end of my crush on Cav. Seriously, what relationship could come back from something like this? But the part of him that's James, that listened to me, and seemed to care for me, he's what's also giving me hope.

CHAPTER 18

When school gets out, Thomas is waiting for me, leaning against my car.

"You're the last person I'd expect to find waiting for me," I tell him.

He raises an eyebrow. "You'd expect Cav before me?"

I shrug. "I wouldn't put it past him to have another go, without you stopping him this time."

He runs a hand through his blond hair. It flops right back in his eyes, and I try to ignore how attractive that move is. "Look, I—"

I hold up a hand. "You don't need to apologize for him. *If*, and that's a big fucking if, he wants to, he can do it himself. He doesn't need you cleaning up his messes."

"I don't clean up his messes."

It's my turn to raise an eyebrow. "No?" I'm tired, I'm sore, and I'm sick of all of this shit.

"Not all the time," he concedes.

"Just *most* of the time?"

He shrugs. "He's my best friend. Isn't that what you're supposed to do for them?"

"Not if they're an ass and you spend most of your time saying 'he didn't mean it' or 'he's not as bad as he seems.'"

He leans fully against my car. "Real talk?" he asks.

I throw my hands up, well, as much as I can with screaming ribs. "Why not."

"Cav's an ass."

I snort. "Tell me something I don't know."

He looks at the blood drops on my shirt, the stiff way I'm holding myself. "Yeah, okay." He scratches the stubble on his cheek. "Look, for some reason, and I don't know what or why, Cav has a problem with you."

"You think?"

"Okay, I guess you knew that."

"Something gave it away."

"So yeah, Cav's an ass. And there's something about you that gets to him. I don't think that's fair."

"Oh, we're talking fairness now?" I ask. "I don't think fairness ever came into this."

"Fair point."

I give him a look.

He cringes. "Sorry. Anyway, as I was saying, I don't like the way he's treating you."

I tilt my head. "Why?"

"Huh?"

"You're his best friend, right? Why are you saying this to me?"

"Like I said, it's not fair. *Cav* isn't fair. To anyone. But least of all to you. Or to me."

"Ah, I get it. It's not so much about how he's treating

me, but because you're looking to use this situation to your advantage."

He shrugs.

I sigh and lean on the car next to him. "What do you want, Thomas?"

"I've never seen Cav like this, like *ever*. You're like his kryptonite. And it's fascinating to me. Why you? You're no one. Sure, you drive a nice car, but Cav's is nicer. Better. Probably faster."

"Well…" I say, not willing to concede that point.

He laughs. "A good businessman takes whatever advantage is presented to him. You're my advantage. I want to be even with Cav. I want to be *better* than Cav. I want all the attention to be on me. I want to be the big man on campus. I want to rule the school. And you're going to help me do it."

"So I'm just a pawn in your quest for power and attention."

He gives me a smirk and shrugs. "Is that so bad?"

"Why would I even go along with something like this? You're best friends with Cavanaugh McLaughlin, you've seen and heard it all and have gone along with it all these years."

"Okay, yeah, I have. But I promise I won't do to you what he's done to you."

"And what's in it for me?"

"Is Cav off your back not enough?"

"Not if it's going to cause me more problems."

He pats my shoulder. Hard. I try to hide my wince but fail miserably. "Sorry. Look, just leave it with me. We'll be friends, it'll be fine. You'll be free of your Cav problem and me, well, I get to have some fun of my own."

I shake my head. "I don't know about this."

"Come on, trust me. I promise I won't let anything happen to you."

I bite my lip. After a while, I nod.

A smile splits Thomas's face. "Excellent." He pats me again, gentler this time. "I'll be in touch."

He turns, then turns back again. "I almost forgot, some of my friends, they race and shit. I could get you in if you wanted."

"I've already said I'm in this… scheme of yours, no need to bribe me."

"Who says this is a bribe?"

"It's not?"

"Call it a… perk."

"And this perk will get me into a super secret illegal street race?"

He laughs. "C'mon, I know you have to be dying to test that R-SPEC out, see what she can do."

"Maybe."

"Like fuck you're not. Here." He hands me his phone. "Gimme your number, and I'll let you know when the next meet is."

I put my number in and hand it back. A few seconds later, my phone buzzes in my pocket. The vibration feels like the nail in my coffin.

He pockets his phone and starts to walk away. "I'll see 'ya round," he calls over his shoulder.

"What was that about?" Jase asks, coming over to me.

"Truthfully? I have no fucking idea."

CHAPTER 19

Being Thomas's whatever is... weird, but he seems to be relishing his newfound role. He's now sitting with Chloe and me at lunch, sending the gossip mill into overdrive. And for the moment, it seems enough to keep Cav away. For that reason alone, I'm willing to go with it, see where it goes and how much it rattles Cav. This is what it's all about, after all. For me, anyway.

"What the fuck have you done to Thomas Rose?" Chloe asks as she drags me away.

"Nothing. Why?"

"Then why the fuck is he sitting with us all of a sudden?"

I shrug. "We're, um, friends."

"*Friends?*" she screeches.

"Yeah, like you and I are."

She shakes her head. "Uh-uh, *not* like we are. We have a genuine connection and mutual goals."

"How do you know Thomas and I don't?" I ask.

"Because he's Thomas Rose, second spawn of Satan

MEGAN LOWE

behind Cavanaugh McLaughlin. How do we know he's not up to something?"

"And if he were?"

She tilts her head. "What are you up to?"

"Nothing. Thomas and I are friends. Truly. He's been watching what Cav has been doing to me and he doesn't like it, so this is him taking a stand against bullying."

"Riiiiiiiiiiiiiiiiight."

"Look, I know you're worried, but you don't need to be."

She quirks an eyebrow. "What if he's trying to get close to you to spy for Cav."

I shrug. "I don't have anything to hide."

"Yeah, but you can get hurt. Again."

I put my hands on her shoulders. "I appreciate the concern, Chlo, I do, but it's not needed."

She chews on her lip.

"It'll be fine."

She sighs and rolls her eyes. "What are you going to do about Cav?" she asks.

I shake my head. "What do I need to do?"

"Oh, honey." She pats my shoulder. "You don't think this will cause waves? It's *already* causing waves. Plus, Cav isn't stupid. He'll figure out what you're doing."

I groan and run my hands through my hair. "I just wanted things to be simple."

I'm swapping my calculus books for my history ones when I'm shoved into my locker, the corner of the door going into my chest. "Ow! What the fuck?" I ask.

"What are you doing with Thomas?" Cav asks.

"We've formed a book club."

"A book club?"

"Yeah, you know, we read books, and then we get together and discuss them. Our current pick is *What If It's Us*. It's about two boys who fall in love in New York. Very touching story, but funny too. I highly recommend it."

"You think you're funny, don't you?"

I sigh and take a deep breath. I need to be cool, calm, and collected. Antagonizing Cav isn't going to help anything. I hold up my hand in apology.

"I want you to leave Thomas alone."

"Once again, I'm not doing anything. He came to *me*. If he wants to spend time with me and my friend, that's his choice."

"He's *my* best friend."

"Never said he wasn't. He still is, by the way."

"What's he doing with you? Why is he with you?"

"You can ask him, you know."

He grits his teeth.

I sigh and lean against my locker. "I think, if you *were* to ask him, he'd tell you he's taking a stand against bullying."

"And if I ask you?"

"I'd say he's trying, in his own way, maybe the only way he knows how, to make my life even a tiny bit easier." I lower my voice. "I'm not your enemy, Cav. I don't want to make trouble for you. I didn't want to make trouble even *before* I knew who you were. But I meant what I said in my texts. This is a good thing. A *great* thing. A wondrous thing even. We found each other. Despite everything. In spite of all the men in this city, we. Found. Each. Other."

He pushes me away.

"I told you I don't know what you're talking about."

I nod. "Okay. Fine. But I do. And I won't forget. I *can't* forget." I give him a smile.

He opens his mouth, but doesn't say anything. It's only when someone walks a little too close by, that our bubble pops.

"What is your problem, fag?"

I sigh and my shoulders drop.

"I'm not who you think I am," he tells me.

I grab his hand and lift it. "This scar says you're *exactly* who I think you are. Who you could be, if you wanted to be." And I do want him to be. *So* badly. I didn't imagine what we had. I didn't make it up. It was real. It *could* be real, if only he wanted it to be.

He rips his hand out of mine. "Tell me again what Thomas is doing with you."

I shrug. "We're hanging out, doing things that friends do."

"What sort of things are you talking about?" he asks.

I sigh and lean back against the lockers. "He's not spilling your secrets, if that's what you're worried about. And I'm not either."

"You don't know any of my secrets."

"Fine, whatever."

"Just leave him alone," he says.

I throw my hands up. Cool, calm, and collected be damned. This... man is so freaking infuriating. "I'm not doing anything to him!" I yell. "I didn't take him from you, and I sure as shit am not telling him he can't be friends with us both. And FYI, this whole thing is *so* incredibly childish."

"He was my friend first."

"He's *still* your friend; his horizons are just expanding. Jesus Christ. What's going to happen when you go off to college? You going to carry him around in your pocket then too? What happens if he gets a girlfriend? You going to be there, sitting on the end of the bed, watching as he has sex with her?"

"Isn't that more your thing?" he asks. "Or do you just lead people on?"

A smile pulls at my lips. "I don't lead anyone on. I also don't hide or pretend to be someone I'm not."

He clenches his fists. "So that girl the other day knew the deal with you then?"

"What girl?" I ask. Then I remember EJ coming and perching on my lap. I laugh. "She was no one. *Is* no one." Then it clicks. "Oh my God, you're jealous."

"Fuck off."

"Is that why you wouldn't talk to me that night? Because you saw us talking? Her coming on to me? Surely you knew that she didn't mean anything." I can't deny that my heart skips a little beat hearing that. He cares. Deep down, probably *very* deep down, he cares. Cav cares.

"I don't give a shit what you do."

"No?" Emboldened by what he just said, I sidle up to him, close enough that I can feel the heat radiating from his body. I run my hand down his chest, to his belt, then lower, cupping him lightly. It might be wishful thinking, or perhaps my overactive imagination, but I *swear* he jerks under my touch. "You telling me this has never got hard for me? You've never jerked it to me, never thought about me at all?"

He slams me against the lockers, my head bouncing off the metal. "Why the fuck would I *ever* get off on you?"

"Please don't hide from me," I beg. I hate how needy, how desperate I sound, but this is what he does to me. This is what he turns me into. This is what I'm willing to do for him.

"You need to drop it," he tells me.

"Why won't you talk to me? We used to be able to tell each other anything. We told each other everything. Why can't we be like we used to be?"

"Why does it matter so much to you what I do?"

"Why *doesn't* it matter to you?" I counter. "This is who you are, Cav. You shouldn't have to hide it."

"You don't understand."

"If I remember correctly, I told you I want to, that you could talk to me about *anything*. You said the same to me, and I more than took advantage, remember?" He stays silent. "And you know what?" I continue. "It helped. A *lot*. Being able to get what I was thinking and feeling off my chest made me feel *so* much better. I know it would work for you too."

He shakes his head. "Nothing can help me."

I cup his cheek, but he pulls away. "That's not true. Let me in," I beg. "Let me help. *Please*."

"No." He picks me up and slams me against the lockers again.

"Cav!" Thomas yells, pushing through the crowd neither of us noticed building. He gets between the two of us, prying Cav's hands away from my chest. "What the fuck are you doing?"

"What am *I* doing?" Cav asks. "What the fuck are *you* doing?"

"He's my friend," Thomas replies.

"I thought *I* was your friend."

"I can have more than one."

"Don't even bother," I tell Thomas. "I've tried and tried to tell him that, but he won't listen to me."

Thomas throws his head back and laughs. "Cav, man, I'm just making friends, talking to Connor here about that sweet R-SPEC he's got in the parking lot. I'm going to get him to test it out in the Skids next month."

Cav's head swings to mine. "You're driving in the Skids?"

I shrug. Truthfully, I hadn't decided if I was going to compete or just watch.

According to Thomas, the Skids is an underground street racing circuit. Meets are sporadic, and the location always changes. Pink slips or cash are the usual prizes.

I went to a couple of meets like this in Michigan, when a few friends and I went down to Detroit. I'm not going to lie, the thought of racing scares me a little, but by equal measure, it also excites me. I love fast cars, and what's the point of having one of the best and not showing it off?

"Why would you tell him about that?" Cav asks Thomas.

"Why wouldn't I?" he replies. "You've seen his ride. A car like that is screaming out for an opportunity to show what it can do."

"He won't be able to handle it," Cav says.

"How do you know?" Thomas asks as I say, "Ah, I think that's up to me to decide and prove you wrong."

"This isn't like *The Fast and the Furious*," Cav says. "These guys don't fuck around."

"I never thought it was," I tell him. "And this isn't my first rodeo, you know."

He laughs. "You think that whatever they have back in bumfuck, Ohio—"

"Michigan," I correct.

"Whatever. You think whatever they have there can compare to here?"

"I don't know if you know this or not, but Detroit is also known as Motor City. There are a *lot* of cars around. There are also a lot of races. I'm betting we hold our own."

He stares at me, jaw clenched, eyes narrowed.

In the end, he shakes his head. "You have no idea what you're getting yourself into. No idea."

CHAPTER 20

"So what's this talk of you taking Cav on at the Skids?" Jase asks when we get home that night.

"Where the hell'd you hear that?" I ask.

He rolls his eyes. "It's only, like, *all* over school," he tells me. "I mean, I was probably the last to know, so it pretty much guarantees everyone else knows about it."

"Why would you be the last to know?" I question.

"Er, because I have, like, no friends."

"I thought you said you were making some?"

"Making and keeping are two different things," he tells me. "It's okay though; I don't mind being alone."

"I mind."

"What are you going to do, Con?" he asks. "Go up to all my teachers, demand that they make people be my friend? I don't think so."

"Why don't they like you? You're great."

"You have to say that; you're my brother."

"I'd say it even if I weren't because it's true."

"Whatever."

"So why don't people like you?"

He shrugs. "I dunno. I'm not like them. I don't care about computer games or seeing how much weed or booze I can steal off my older siblings or parents, and that's all they care about."

"What about the girls?" I ask.

"They only care about makeup palettes and push-up bras. Not exactly my areas of expertise."

I sigh and hug him. "I'm sorry. High school sucks. What can I say?"

He laughs. "At least you've only got this year left."

"Do you think a new school would be different?"

He shrugs. "Probably not. It's just…. When you've watched both of your parents struggle to breathe, what people my age are into, it all seems a bit… insignificant."

I nod. "I guess it would."

"But it's cool. I just keep my head down and do my work. I'm sitting on mostly A's, so that's good."

"That's awesome, Jase."

"I figure if I can get into a good college and make the right connections, in twenty or so years I'll be all the douchebags' boss and be able to treat *them* like shit."

I laugh. "That's some plan."

He shrugs. "It's all I've got right now."

"You know, if things get too bad, you can always come to me. Chloe would have no problem with you hanging out with us. Might even be able to show everyone up because you're hanging with seniors."

"Thanks, but I don't need my big brother fighting my battles for me."

"Who's fighting them *for* you? I'll fight them *with* you."

He nods. "So are you going to tell me what's up with you and Cav now?"

I blow out a breath. "I was hoping you'd forgotten about that."

"Not likely. You're really going to race him?"

"I don't know. Thomas told me about some races, and I thought I'd go and check them out. I hadn't decided on whether I was going to race, and I especially hadn't decided if I was going to race Cav."

"That would be awesome, though."

The look on Cav's face when Thomas first mentioned the Skids comes into my head. Anger, frustration, and maybe a *bit* of concern marred his features, but also gets my blood pumping.

"Yeah, it would be," I agree.

"So who's this Thomas guy?" Jase asks. "Is he nice? Someone I should know about?"

"You telling me you don't already know about Thomas Rose?"

He chuckles. "Only what I've heard at school, that he's Cav's best friend and does his bidding. Sounds like a stand-up guy." He rolls his eyes, and I give him a playful shove.

"He's nice," I say.

"Nice like nice or *nice*?"

"Just nice. Things aren't like that."

"Because you don't like him like that?"

"Not every guy is boyfriend material."

"*Boyfriend material?*" His voice gets dangerously high.

"You know what I mean."

"So you like Thomas, but just as friends."

"Yeah." I nod. "That's not to say he's not nice to look at, because he is."

We both chuckle.

"Is the reason you don't like him because you're stuck on Cav?"

I blow out a breath. "I don't know. I mean, I don't think Thomas is gay, so that may have something to do with it."

"*Are* you still stuck on Cav?" he asks.

"I'm trying not to be, but…."

"But you do really like him."

"Is that stupid?"

"Yes."

"Geez, don't hold back now, bud."

He shrugs. "You asked." He puts his hand on my shoulder. "Look, I get you like a dark, mysterious, brooding bad boy, but from what I hear, Cavanaugh McLaughlin is a nasty piece of work. You don't want to be caught in his web. *I* don't want you caught in his web."

I run a hand through my hair. "You're right."

"But there is something about him," he continues.

I chuckle. "Yeah, there is."

"Look, I know I'm only fifteen and don't know shit, really, but I think if Cav is on your mind, then maybe there's a reason for that?"

"Like fate or something?"

He shrugs. "Yeah, maybe."

"You think that's a thing?"

"I think it is if you want it to be. Look, Con, I'm not going to turn around and tell you not to pursue this thing with Cav. One, you have no reason to listen to me, and two, even if you did, I know you wouldn't."

I nod.

"*But* if you think there's something worth pursuing with Cav, then go for it."

"Do you think he'll let me?"

"*Let* you?"

"You know, be open to being with me."

He shrugs. "I don't know. I think he has one heck of a reputation at Windswept, and being with you would be a massive shock to that."

I nod.

"I think what you have to do is convince him that you're worth it."

"Do you think it will be?"

"Only you can answer that. As your brother, I'm always going to back your decision and choices. Do I think Cav is the right guy for you? Not particularly, but I'm open to seeing what you see."

"You think I'm an idiot."

"I think the Cav you know and the Cav I know are *very* different people."

I sigh and nod. "I don't know what to do," I tell him.

He pats my shoulder. "Maybe you're not supposed to. Maybe you're supposed to follow your gut and go with it."

"Go with it, right." I can totally do that.

CHAPTER 21

A week on from Jase and my conversation and I still don't know what my gut is telling me about Cav. Thomas is still hanging out with us, and Cav is still shooting me dirty looks but hasn't done anything about it. Yet. I'm not stupid enough to think it's not coming. I know it is; I just have to be prepared to act when it does. But at least I have Thomas to help me when he does. So far, things are okay. I think he's waiting for Cav to make the first move. It'll look better that way, if Cav attacks. In the meantime though, life goes on.

"Hey, so I hear Navy Pier is doing something this weekend. You know, one last party before winter hits," Chloe says at lunch.

Thomas nods. "They're opening the bridges on Saturday so the boats can get to dry dock. It's pretty cool to watch."

"Jase and I are going to be inside one of those bridge house things, you know, watch the gears raise the bridges," I tell them.

"No shit?" Thomas asks.

"No shit," I reply.

"I've always wanted to see that."

"We got tickets ages ago. It was nuts trying to get them, but we're both into mechanics and engineering so it was worth the hassle."

"Sounds scintillating," Chloe says, rolling her eyes. I give her a playful shove.

"It is actually pretty interesting," Thomas says.

"Thank you."

"You're welcome."

"See?" I poke my tongue out at Chloe.

"Anyway," she says, talking over the top of us. "Saturday night? Navy Pier?"

"I dunno. I promised Jase we'd spend the day together. We'll do the bridge thing, then head to Wildberry for some pancakes and then maybe hit up Sears Tower."

"Touristy shit."

I shrug. "We're from Michigan. We haven't done that stuff before. Besides, he's having a bit of a hard time at the moment. I want to make sure he's all right, that he knows I'm there for him."

Thomas puts his hand over mine. "I'm sure he does."

I look down at our hands, bringing Thomas's attention to it. He removes it like he was burned. There's been more and more of these sorts of innocent touches between us lately. I don't quite understand what he's doing. I don't think he's interested in me, and there's no way he can know that Cav/James and I had a... whatever it is we had, so what is his end game?

"Sorry," he mutters.

I wave it off. "It's fine."

"Just bring him to the Pier," Chloe says, glaring at Thomas's hand. "It's the last real blowout before we all start freezing our asses off."

"You know, I wouldn't have thought Navy Pier was your thing."

She shrugs. "It's all about the people you go with. It probably is pretty lame, but I have no doubt we all could have some fun."

"Then let's have some fun," I say. "I'm pretty sure we could all use it."

"That was *awesome*," Jase says as we exit the bridge house and walk along the river for a bit, watching the boats sail past.

"It was pretty cool," I agree. As much as I love Michigan, the architectural look and feel of Chicago is right up my alley.

We walk for a bit, both content with our own thoughts before I break that.

"So, ah, how's school?" I ask.

Jase groans.

"What?"

He looks at me. "Really?"

"What?" I ask again. "It's a legit and warranted question."

"You really want to ruin what's going on right now by asking about *school*?"

"That good, huh?"

He shrugs. "It is what it is."

"And just what is it exactly?"

"It's high school, Con. It's not supposed to be good except for like, twelve people."

"And you're not one of the twelve."

He shrugs again. "It's totally fine. I've only got three-and-three-quarter years left."

"A lot could change in that time."

"Yeah, maybe."

"Is there, um, anyone in particular who's being, um, particularly horrible?"

"What are you gonna do?" he asks. "Go to Principal Rowling? Or maybe you'll go to Amy, seeing as though you two are all good now, and *she* can go to the school."

I stop him with a hand on his arm. "Whoa. Where is this coming from?"

He throws up his hands. "You can't fight my battles for me, Con."

"I told you before, I don't want to fight them *for* you, I want—"

"To fight them with me, yeah, I got that."

"So why won't you let me?"

"Because it's just as bad. Oh, look at little Jase, he needs his older brother to come fight his battles with him."

"Is that what people are saying?"

"No, but they will."

"How do you know that?" I ask.

"I just do, okay?"

I grab him by the shoulders. "No, it's not okay. You're having a hard time, and I want to be there for you, help you through it if I can."

"And if you can't?"

"Then I'm going to die trying."

Jase's face pales.

"Shit. I didn't mean it like that. I mean, I'm going to do everything I possibly can to help you get through this, okay? It's you and me, just like it always has been."

He nods.

"Now, you want to tell me why you're pissed me and Amy and have sort of figured out our shit?"

He scuffs the toe of his sneaker into the ground. "Not really."

"Seems that's a common theme today," I muse.

He shrugs yet again. "So?"

"So it pisses me off. It doesn't do any good to bottle shit up, Jase. You know that."

"What are you? My therapist?"

"Nope, just the older brother who's been through everything you're going through. Remember that?"

He looks up at me, eyes blazing. "Yeah, I do. Do you?"

I rear back a little. "Of course I do."

"But you're more than happy to ditch me for Amy anyway."

"Hey, hey, hey," I say. "Who said I'm ditching you?" I look around. "I don't see her here now, do I? She's not hiding in the bushes somewhere, is she?"

He mumbles something under his breath.

"I'm sorry, I didn't catch that," I tell him.

He shakes his head. "It doesn't matter," he says. "Just like me." He mumbles the last bit.

"Who the fuck said you don't matter?" I demand. "Who, Jase?" I ask when he doesn't answer.

"It's what'll happen," he says. "You're finishing school

141

soon, and you and Amy will be free to do whatever you want, and I'll be stuck here."

"First off," I say, "technically Amy is free to do what she wants *now*. I know she hasn't always been here for us, but she *is* trying. Secondly, I'm eighteen, legally an adult, which means I too am technically free to do what I want, but no matter where I am, I will *always* be here for you if you want me to or not. Even if I manage to get my ass accepted into some college somewhere."

Mom was an alumnus at UM, but Dad went to Northwestern, just like Amy did. I know if I want to go there, I've got a legacy spot, the same as Jase will too.

I hug him tight. "Just because Amy and I have sort of, and I stress *sort of* worked out our differences doesn't mean we'll forget you or ignore you or leave you out. In fact, you're probably the only thing we have in common, besides, you know, DNA."

He chuckles and clings to me tighter. "It's just hard sometimes," he says. "I miss them so much. I miss my friends, my old school, everything. You've got new friends and have fixed things with Amy, and what do I have? Nothing."

"You have me," I tell him. "You will *always* have me."

He nods.

"And I promise things will get better at school. Come sit with us. I dare anyone to say anything, okay?"

He nods. "Thanks, Con."

I press a kiss to the top of his head. "You never have to thank me. Ever."

CHAPTER 22

After a filling meal of gigantic pancakes at Wildberry and awesome views of Chicago from the top of Sears/Willis Tower, Jase and I head to Navy Pier.

"Are you sure it's okay I'm tagging along?" he asks for the fifty-seventh time.

I ruffle his hair. "It is *way* more than okay. I told the guys what we were doing, and they said to invite you as well."

"So this wasn't your idea?"

"Wha—? Of course it was. I mean…." I stop when he bursts out laughing. "You jackass," I say as I grab him around the neck and run my knuckles over the top of his head.

"Ow! Get off me!"

I laugh as I let him go.

"You should've seen your face," he says as he tidies his hair.

"I never want you thinking you're anything less than my number-one priority, okay?"

"Yeah, okay."

"Come on, let's have some fun."

I have to admit, when Chloe first mentioned this, I totally thought it would be lame as fuck, but it's not.

"Cheese and caramel is not a combination I thought would work, but I have to admit, this popcorn is pretty good," I say as I shovel another handful into my mouth.

"Excuse you," Chloe says. "How dare you doubt our popcorn expertise?"

"We're from Michigan," I remind them, gesturing between Jase and me. "We're bred to *hate* you guys. Of course we're gonna doubt your popcorn flavors."

They all shake their heads.

"Isn't this cozy?" a voice says from behind us.

"Cav!" Thomas says, "I didn't think this would be your scene."

"You know I go where the action is," Cav replies. "And it looks like I found *all* the action." He looks Jase up and down. I step in front of my brother while Cav laughs.

Thomas looks around. "Why are you here by yourself? Where's everyone else?"

He shrugs. "Maybe I'm confident enough to go out on my own."

Thomas nods. "How very progressive of you."

He spreads his arms wide. "I'm nothing but a modern man."

I snort. Coming from the guy who is too afraid to

come out as gay, even to himself. "Why are you here, Cav?" I ask.

"Am I not allowed to come here looking for a good time?"

"And what sort of good time would that be?" Again, the words are out of my mouth before I realize what I'm saying.

"Little Siddell," he says to Jase. "How's it hanging?"

"Don't answer him," I say to my brother.

"Aw, why not?" Cav asks. "I'm not going to hurt him."

"No, you just hurt me."

"Don't worry, I'm sure being the good brother he is, he'd never *dream* of betraying you, would he?"

Thomas pinches the bridge of his nose. "I didn't betray you, Cav."

"Says you."

"Just leave Thomas and my brother alone," I say. "Neither of them is interested in playing your games."

He chuckles. "Who says I'm playing?"

"Cav...."

Cav ignores both of us and speaks directly to Jase. "If you ever get tired of your brother's overbearing shit, you know where to find me."

"Just get out of here, Cav," Thomas says. "We just wanted to have a nice night out."

"And I don't?"

"Do you? *Really?*"

"I'm here. Why else would I be?"

"Oh, I don't know," Chloe says. "Maybe to cause shit?"

He gives a butter-wouldn't-melt smile, and I swear my heart skips a beat. "Would I do that?"

"Just go home, Cav," I tell him.

"B-but I j-just want to be p-part of the c-cool g-g-group." He mock pouts. "I-I don't h-have any f-fr-friends and you h-have *so* many."

I roll my eyes.

He points to Jase. "I bet he buys it."

I shove him, my hands against his chest. "Leave. Him. Out. Of. It."

"It sucks when someone you care about is targeted, isn't it?" he asks.

"The only difference is I didn't target Thomas. He came to me."

He shoves me away. "Yo, little Siddell," he calls as he walks away. "If you ever need a friend, you can come to me. I promise I won't ruin your reputation like your brother here will."

"Shut up, Cav," I hiss.

He laughs. "Enjoy your... fun."

"That guy gives me the shits," Chloe says. "Like, majorly."

"I'm so sorry," Thomas apologizes. "I didn't know he'd be here."

"Which brings us to an interesting point. What *are* you doing with us? I'm not buying your I-want-to-be-the-good-guy act."

"I can't be friends with you guys?" he asks.

"No, not really," she replies. "Cav has made it more than clear what he thinks of Connor, and he's never really bothered with me before, so why all the sudden interest from you?"

"I'm not Cav. Just because he likes or doesn't like something or someone doesn't mean I have to follow."

"But you usually do, don't you?" She folds her arms across her chest.

"Are you questioning my motives for hanging out with you guys?" he asks.

"That's exactly what I'm doing."

"You don't think he did this too?" He gestures to me.

"I don't care if Connor interrogated you, *I'm* doing it now, and I've got to say, I'm not overly impressed with your answers."

"Guess it's good that your opinion's not the only one that counts then, huh?"

Chloe shakes her head. "You think you're slick, don't you? That because you're the great Thomas Rose, right-hand man to Cavanaugh McLaughlin, that you're untouchable. We don't give a shit about him, and we don't give a shit about you. Now, I'll ask you one more time, why the fuck are you here?"

"I'm here because I feel like shit that for years I've done Cav's bidding. I've been his errand boy and done stuff I hate and hate myself for doing. I'm here because I hate how Cav treats people, especially Connor." He stops and takes a breath. "I don't know, I guess I wanted to try and make things right."

"By being our friend?" she asks, eyebrow arched.

"By showing and proving to you that I'm an okay guy, that I'm not like Cav—or that I'm not anymore."

"Hmm."

He shrugs. "I know it can't excuse what's basically a

147

lifetime of doing the wrong thing, but it's a start, right?"
He looks to me.

"Look," I say, "why don't we leave this how it is. I'm okay with Thomas hanging out with us, but if you're not, Chloe, then, I don't know, we can work something out."

She shakes her head. "He's up to something." She points at Thomas. "And I really don't think you should be involved in whatever it is."

I put my hands on her shoulders. "It's fine. It'll *be* fine."

"I think you're wrong, but I'm your friend so I'll go along with whatever it is you guys are up to. I just hope that when things blow up in your faces, and they will blow up in your faces, you remember that I told you not to do it. You also better pray that things don't get too bad otherwise you'll get hurt. Again. And I don't want that to happen."

"You think I do?"

"I think you're letting a hard body and a pretty face fuck with your thinking. I think you want—" she looks to Thomas, who in turn is watching us closely, "—*things* that aren't possible and that you should just let lie."

"It's nothing," I tell her again. At this point, I don't know who I'm fooling. It's certainly not either of us. This crush I have on Cav... I don't even think it can be called a crush anymore. I want him and apparently, by aligning myself with Thomas, I'm willing to do just about anything to get to him.

She gives me a glare that tells me she's not buying any of my shit.

"Okay, I think that's more than enough excitement for

one night. Why don't we all head home, and we can figure out where we stand on Monday, huh?" I say.

"Whatever," Chloe mutters, before walking off.

"Sorry, dude," Thomas says as we watch her leave. "I didn't want my stuff interfering with your friendships."

"It's fine. She's just looking out for me."

He nods. "What was that she was saying about you wanting things that aren't possible?"

"Oh, nothing."

"Really?" he asks. "'Cause it seemed like something."

I sigh. "I *may* have a teeny, tiny, itsy, bitsy, baby crush on Cav, which is beyond stupid. I know this. He's not interested in me. He's *never* going to be interested in me so I should just let it go."

"Hmm." He scratches his chin.

"And it's not like I haven't been trying to get over it," I say, words pouring out of my mouth now. "I have. But I don't know, I think there's another side to him, a softer one, a more caring one. And I thought I could be the one to bring it out in him. I know it's stupid and something out of a soppy romance novel, but yeah, it's stuck there and I'm trying to get it out but it's hard."

"Especially when he seems to have a fascination with you," Thomas finishes.

I shrug. "I know it'll never, *ever* happen but yeah, he's not making it easy."

"Still," he says, "it is strange that he's so obsessed with you."

"I'm sure it's because he thinks I'm an easy target or something. I'm not really fighting back so I guess I'm playing into his hands."

"Yeah, I'm sure that is it." He has a faraway look in his eyes. He shakes his head. "Anyway, I really did have fun tonight. You guys are awesome."

"Thanks. It was… um, good."

He laughs.

"I know you're worried about Cav, but just leave it with me okay? Tonight gave me some ideas."

"Ah, I don't know."

"Look, you're already in it now, may as well go the whole way. In for a penny, in for a pound, right?"

I scuff my sneaker against the ground. "I just… don't want to get hurt again."

"I can't promise you that you won't. Just like I can't promise that Cav will leave you alone if everything works out the way I want it to. But we have to do something. *You* have to do something." He sighs. "I didn't want to tell you this because I don't want you to worry even more than you already are, but if Cav can't come after you, he might come after Jase. I think that's the logical next step. He's already started laying the groundwork."

I look over to my brother. "What?"

He shrugs. "It's what I'd do. Hit someone where it hurts. It's obvious you care for your brother, and he knows it's probably a weak spot of yours. I hate to break it to you, but you showed that today."

I run my hands through my hair.

"Trust me," he says.

I nod. "Okay."

"I'm not making any promises, and it's entirely likely shit may get worse before it gets better, but I think I understand why he's doing what he's doing and I know what to do about it."

"And you're not going to tell me."

He shakes his head. "No, I'm not. Just trust me that I know what I'm doing and we're going to hit him where it hurts."

I cover my face in my hands. "Fine."

"Good. I'll see you guys on Monday." He waves goodbye before also heading off.

"You have some interesting friends," Jase says as we make our way to the parking lot.

"Yes, yes, I do."

CHAPTER 23

My phone buzzes at some ungodly hour on Sunday, waking me up.

"Hello?" I answer, without looking at who's calling.

"Hey."

"Thomas?" I ask.

"Yeah, sorry. Did I wake you?"

I scrub a hand over my face and look at the clock that reads 10:57 a.m.

"No, it's fine. What's up?"

"I heard from the guy who runs the Skids, Kevin. He told me about a meet this week and I thought I'd let you know."

I sit up. "This week?"

"Yeah, Thursday."

"Isn't it a bit early to be announcing the day? I thought they would keep it secret so the cops wouldn't find out."

"Sometimes he gives me an early heads up."

"Oh."

"Yeah. I told him a buddy of mine had an R-SPEC and was looking to test it out."

"Yeah?" I ask.

"Yeah. He was excited. I don't know if they'll have room for you to race this meet, but maybe the next one?"

"That would be awesome."

"You're sure about racing?"

"Oh yeah, absolutely." I've raced a few times in Detroit and I was hooked. I wanted to take my mom but by that time she was too sick. She would've loved it though. Amy on the other hand, would probably blow a gasket if she knew what I was planning.

He chuckles.

"So what are they like?" I ask. "What's the competition like?"

"Oh man, it's insane. Racing's not my thing, but there is so much there. Every type of car you can think of is there."

"Including a certain Chevy Chevelle SS?"

"Naturally."

"He's not going to let me race, is he?"

"It's not a question of 'let'. He doesn't run the Skids so it's not like he can say absolutely yes or no. But he could make it difficult."

"Why doesn't he want me to race?" I ask.

"That I don't know," he replies. "Usually Cav's all over fresh meat, wanting to show his dominance and all that."

"His dominance?"

"He's the best."

"He's really that good?" I ask.

"Yeah, he is. When he's in the Chevelle, he's impossible

to beat. The time, effort, and money he's put into that car.... It's his pride and joy."

"So you don't think anyone can beat him?"

"Hmm," he considers. "I mean, it's possible. I've just never seen it happen."

"If that's the case, why doesn't he want *me* to race?"

"Like I said, it doesn't make sense. I think I have an idea, but I could be wrong."

"Ready to share with the class?" I ask.

He chuckles again. "Not really. You, um, never met Cav before you started at Windswept, did you?"

"How would I meet him? I moved here like a month before school started. I knew no one and knew even less about the city." Technically, I'm telling the truth. I never met James, we just talked. And mutually masturbated. But we never met.

"Right."

"Why?"

"Oh, it's nothing. I just have a suspicion about Cav and I thought you might be able to either let me know I was on the right track or not."

"Me? How?"

"Don't worry, it's probably nothing."

"You don't really think that, though, do you?"

He sighs. "No, I don't."

"So why do you think I could help confirm things for you?" I ask. There's only one way I could help and that's....

"It's probably nothing. I'll just have to go in another angle," he says.

"What do you know?" I ask.

"It's just something I have a hunch on. It's fine, I'll find another way."

"Um, okay."

"So the Skids, Thursday night, I'll swing by and we can go together."

"I-If you want."

"Yeah, it would probably be best."

"They don't just let in any riff raff off the street?" I ask.

"No. I mean, they don't, but that's not why we should go together."

"And you're not going to let me in on that reason either?"

"It'll just look better."

Figuring that's as much as I'm going to get, I take it. "Okay then."

"I know this all very secretive. I swear I'm not doing it on purpose, but it's really for the best. Our end game here is to bring down Cav, right?"

"Yeah, sure."

"And we'll get there, I just need you to trust me. I know I haven't given you a reason to, but I'm on your side. I want to bring him down as much as you do."

"Yeah, I know."

"It'll work, I promise. You get to him. I think I know why, so we're close."

"Okay."

"I'll let you go, but I'll see you on Monday."

"Yup, Monday."

"It's all good, Connor. Don't worry."

Famous last words.

CHAPTER 24

I've been to races in Detroit and thought they were pretty impressive. They are nothing, *nothing* compared to the Skids.

"Holy shit," Jase whispers as we drive in.

"Right?" Thomas asks from the back seat. "It's insane, isn't it?"

"It's something," I reply.

"Is this what heaven looks like?" Jase asks.

"A certain type of person's heaven, I guess," Thomas replies.

It's just as he described: every type of car you can think of, all done up to an incredibly impressive standard.

"Let's park and walk around," Thomas suggests.

I nod and find a spot, several heads turning as we drive past.

"This is just the posturing," Thomas explains as we walk around. "People showing what they've got under the hood, others deciding who they want to go up against."

"What sort of races are they?" I ask.

"Depends. Sometimes they're a flat quarter mile, other times it can be a couple of mile street circuit."

"Open roads?"

He shrugs. "Can't close several miles of road."

"Wow," Jase says.

"Do you ever race?" I ask.

He shrugs again. "Sometimes. I mean, I like cars, but that's it. They're just cars. I'm not in love with them, not like—"

"Like Cav," I finish.

He chuckles. "And you." He shoves me playfully.

"It's a passion."

"And I just don't have it. It doesn't bother me. I still like coming here, watching the races, looking at the cars. I don't see something someone else has done and go, okay, I *have* to do that to my car. How many ideas have you had just now?"

"A few," I admit. The Mustang is incredible as it is, and I have made some minor changes, but there's always room for more.

"See? We're not the same, but it's all good."

We walk around a bit more, Jase quiet, taking everything in.

A little while later, Thomas introduces me to Kevin, the "unofficial" organizer of the whole thing.

"You interested in racing?" he asks me. "I've seen one R-SPEC in action, and it was a beauty."

"No," a voice answers for me. "He's not interested."

Cav comes over and shakes Kevin's hand.

"The fuck I'm not," I rebut. In school I might be wary of taking him on, but here? This is my lifeblood, my passion. I know what I'm doing here. Here, he can't take anything from me and I won't let him.

"This isn't some hick town race pretending to be the real thing. This *is* the real thing; we don't play around here."

"Good, I don't either."

He raises an eyebrow and folds his arms across his chest. "No?" I try to ignore just how good Cav looks out of uniform, but, fuck, he does. His chest is broad and strong, his tattoos that I so rarely get to see at school on full display. The design's full of smoke, and stars, and dragons, and roses. It makes a guy want to do things. Bad things.

"No more than you do."

At that, he throws his head back and laughs.

"Seriously, man, what is your problem?" I ask.

He shakes his head. "There's no problem."

"Really?"

"Really."

"So why don't you want me to race?"

"Because I don't want amateurs out there. They're dangerous. Racing is dangerous, and I very much like living, thank you very much."

"I know how to race," I tell him.

"You'd be open to doing a trial race?" Kevin asks.

I shrug. "Sure."

Cav's jaw clenches, and he balls his fists, his hands now at his sides.

"No," he says again.

I throw my hands up.

"Cav, man, it's cool. We'll have everything set up as well as we can; it'll be fine," Kevin says.

"What are you afraid of?" I ask him.

"I told you, that you'll hurt or kill someone."

"And I've said I'm willing to prove my skill level. But here's a newsflash for you: even experienced drivers make mistakes. I bet you've made your fair share."

"Oh shit, do you remember that race against the Aston Martin?" Thomas asks. "You oversteered coming into the corner and almost took the both of you out."

"Shut up, Thomas," Cav snaps.

"So the god does make mistakes," I say.

He shrugs. "Shit happens. It's how you come back from them that counts."

Thomas nods. "That's *exactly* right," he says. "I mean, we all make mistakes, all do things I'm sure we regret."

Cav looks at him, his brows pinched. "Riiiiight."

Clearly I'm not the only one who doesn't know where Thomas is going with this.

"But it's our friends who can help with that, can't they?"

"Ah, sure."

I'm totally and utterly lost by now.

"Because they're what *really* matters."

"What the fuck are you on?" Cav asks, seemingly sick of Thomas's weird tangent.

He laughs. It's fake as hell and leaves a whole heap of tension in its wake. "You know me, Cav. I'm just here for a good time."

Cav shakes his head then looks to Kevin. "I don't want

him racing." He throws his thumb over his shoulder to me.

"I guess it's a good thing you don't get a say, then, isn't it?" Thomas asks. "We don't always get what we want, do we?"

"Look, Cav, man," Kevin says. "If he proves himself and he's all right, what's the harm? Plus, that car's a thing of beauty. Don't you want to see what she can do?"

"I don't want him racing," he repeats.

"Why not?" Jase bursts out. "Afraid Connor will beat you?"

"Jase," I hiss. "Stay out of it." The last thing I want, especially after Thomas's warning, is Cav's attention on him.

Cav looks from me to my brother, flexing his hands. Finally, he turns his attention to Jase. "You sick of living in your brother's shadow?" he asks. "Sick of living under his thumb?"

"Leave him out of this," I tell Cav.

"I can't. He's in it now."

"Hardly."

"Try not at all."

He laughs.

"Get lost," I tell him. "I'm going to race, and then we'll see who's the better out of the two of us."

He chuckles as he walks away. "Yeah, maybe."

"I don't know what the fuck just went on," Kevin says once Cav is out of sight, "but if you want to race, we'll give you a trial, and if that goes well, you'll be in permanently."

"Thanks, I appreciate it," I tell him, shaking the hand he offers.

"We've got a full roster tonight, but next meet, you'll be on."

I nod. "Looking forward to it."

"And, ah, this thing you and Cav have got going on, is it going to be a problem?"

I shrug. "Not for me, but him on the other hand…."

He nods. "I'll talk to him."

"Good luck with that."

He gives me a kind smile.

"But, um, what happens if he can't get past whatever's eating at him?"

Kevin runs a hand through his hair. "Let's cross that bridge when we come to it, okay? I'll give you your fair shot, and we can go from there."

"Sounds like a plan."

He nods. "So for tonight, have a look around, get a feel for things, and next time out, we'll see what you and that R-SPEC can do."

"We won't disappoint."

"That's what I'm thinking. Enjoy your night, fellas," he says before walking off.

I blow out a breath.

"Well, that was interesting," Jase says.

I chuckle. "Just a bit."

"But it's cool they're letting you race."

"They're letting me *try out*," I correct.

"Are you sure it's what you want to do?"

I scratch the scruff on my cheek. "I mean, I'm not

saying I'll race every meet, but it would be nice to wipe that smug-ass grin off Cav's face."

"He's scared of you," he says.

"He should be."

Jase rolls his eyes. "I don't mean on the track."

"Neither did I," I reply. "And while I love you trying to back me up, I don't want you anywhere near Cavanaugh McLaughlin, okay? He's my problem, and I don't want you dragged into something you shouldn't be."

"Come on, Con—"

"No. This is between Cav and me. I don't want you anywhere near it."

"Gah!"

"You saw that look in his eyes tonight, Jase. He'll come after you in order to get to me. I don't want that to happen."

"You don't think I can handle him? He doesn't scare me, you know."

"I have no doubt you can handle him," I tell him. "But it's a matter of should you have to? The answer is no. It's my mess. I should be the one to deal with it."

"But I want to help," he insists.

I put a hand on his shoulder. "I know you do, but that's not how this relationship works. I'm the big brother; I protect you. You're the younger brother who's a pain in my and Amy's asses and who makes jokes."

"Sure, that's all I'm good for," he grumbles.

I sling my arm around his neck. "It is *not* all you're good for, but it's all I want you to worry about, okay?"

He nods. "Okay."

CHAPTER 25

What is now our group is sitting at our normal lunch table when Jase comes over.

"C-can I s-sit with y-you g-guys?" he stammers.

I pat the bench beside me. "You know you're always welcome," I tell him. "But why now?"

He wipes at his nose. "Nothing. I-I just f-felt l-like s-sitting here."

Chloe flashes him a dazzling smile. "We always welcome good-looking guys to come and sit with us."

"He's underage," I remind her. "And not even close to your type."

She pokes her tongue out at me. "I was *trying* to be nice."

"T-thanks, Chloe," Jase stammers, although I think this is more from embarrassment than whatever trauma forced him here.

"You're welcome, sweetie."

"Now, are you going to tell me why you're here?" I ask.

He sighs. "It's nothing."

"Yet, I've invited you to sit here a ton of times and you've always said things aren't that bad, which leads me to think they must be if you're here."

"Can't you just leave it?" he asks.

"No."

"I don't know if you've met your brother," Chloe says, "but once he gets an idea in his head, he doesn't drop it."

"I really do hate you," he tells me.

"One of these days you'll realize it all comes from a place of love."

He sighs again. "I'm having trouble with one of the guys in my gym class. It's no big deal, I just don't feel like dealing with it today, so I thought I'd take you up on the offer."

"Who's the guy?" I ask.

"*Please* don't make it worse."

I hold my hands up. "Would I do that?"

He stares at me. "Yes, you would."

"If I promise I won't make it worse, will you tell me?"

"Promise?"

I cross my heart. "On Kris Bryant's life."

The Cubs fans at the table gasp.

"You better not fuck up," Chloe says, pointing a manicured finger at me.

"His name is Simon Brewer," Jase says.

"And what did he do, and why was today particularly brutal?"

"He just likes to give me a hard time, and I can't take it anymore."

"Is he saying anything in particular?" I ask.

"Just the usual shit."

"Help me out, Jase. What in particular?"

"He just says shit like I'm so horrible our parents died to get away from me, that sort of stuff."

I see red. "Which one is he?"

"You said you wouldn't do anything," Jase reminds me.

"No, I said I wouldn't make things *worse*, and I'm not going to. I'm going to make them better." I stand up.

I walk over to what I hope is a table of freshmen. "Simon Brewer. Who is he? Where's he at?"

One of the nerdier guys nearby points to a table near the door. "T-the one with the r-red hair."

I spot him easily. Flaming red hair, covered in freckles, pasty white skin, and gangly limbs.

"Thanks," I say as I march over there, Jase's pleas falling on deaf ears.

I'm at the end of his table, a few feet from him, when Cav bursts in, looks around, and goes straight for... Simon Brewer.

"Yo, Brewer," he says, grabbing him by the collar and pulling him out of his seat.

"W-What?" Brewer replies.

"I hear you're giving a friend of mine a hard time."

"N-No, I w-wouldn't d-d-do t-th-that."

"No? So why did I see you giving Jase Siddell a hard time in the hall as I was going to see Mr. Jansen?" Cav asks.

My feet are frozen to the floor. Why is he doing this? Why now? What's his goal here?

"I-I d-didn't k-know he w-w-was y-your f-friend," Simon says.

"But you do admit to giving him a hard time."

"I-I d-didn't mean i-it."

"Have you apologized?"

Simon shakes his head.

"Jase," Cav calls. "Come here for a sec. Simon has something he wants to say to you."

Jase walks over, shooting me a glance. I shrug in response. I have no earthly idea what the fuck is happening right now, or *why* it's happening.

"Simon?" Cav asks.

"Um, yeah, sorry," he mumbles.

Cav shakes him. "For what?" he asks.

"Um, for what I, um, said, you know, before."

"Just before?"

Simon rolls his eyes. "For everything I've said to you."

"That's more like it," he says.

Finally, my feet unstick themselves and I walk over to Cav, pulling him away. "What the fuck do you think you're doing?" I ask.

He smirks. "Clearly, what you couldn't."

"I was on my way over to confront the little prick when you interrupted."

"Funny, but I don't remember interrupting anything but little Simon there eating his lunch."

"I was on my way," I say, "but that's details. Why are you doing this? And are you seriously going to pull my brother into whatever it is you have against me?"

"I can't try to right a wrong?" he asks. "Bullying is against the school's code of conduct, you know."

"It's never stopped you before," I mutter. "And I highly doubt you're worried about people who go against the code of conduct."

He pats my cheek. "On the contrary, *Con*," he sneers. "What goes on at this school is of great importance to me. Especially when it comes to our new and vulnerable students."

"Jase isn't vulnerable, and we've been here for a few months now. We're hardly new."

"New? Maybe not. But vulnerable? Definitely."

"Vulnerable to whom?" I ask.

He leans in and whispers in my ear. "To me." He leans back. "I told you not to fuck with my friends."

I throw my hands up. "I keep telling you I didn't, so now you're going after my brother because you're too stubborn to listen to what I've told you."

"Why should I listen to you?"

"I've never lied to you," I tell him. "I know you can't say the same to me."

"I didn't lie about everything," he says quietly. "But you took something from me, so it's only fair I take something from you."

I shake my head. "You're a sick and twisted bastard."

He shrugs. "Eh."

"It won't work, you know." This is despite it already working. Thomas warned me that Cav would go after Jase, and I did warn him, but honestly? I never thought Cav would actually go through with it. I didn't think he would sink this low. But Jase is strong. He can handle himself, no matter how much I want to think he can't, that he needs me to fight his battles. He's told me time and time again that he doesn't, but I never listen. It'll be fine. It will all be completely, and utterly, fine.

"Then what do you have to worry about?" he asks.

169

"Unless you are, indeed, worried. Things not so rosy at home, Con? Jase's smile not as bright and just a little bit fake? He having trouble here?" He laughs. "I can see you thinking, figuring, wondering. Good, keep doing that."

"He hasn't done anything to you," I grit out.

"No, he hasn't," he agrees. "But his brother has."

I shake my head, a sadness in my chest. "What have I done to you except tell you I want to be with you?" I ask.

"You showed me what it could be like and I hate you for that," he says before walking over to Jase.

There are big smiles on both their faces, and they do the slap handshake and bro hug thing.

I never thought Cav would stoop this low. But he's not serious, he can't be. Going after me is one thing, but going after my brother?

The look on his face as he embraces Jase tells me he's serious.

But Jase wouldn't be stupid enough to fall for Cav's tricks. Would he?

CHAPTER 26

Apparently the faith I placed in my kid brother was misplaced. It turns out, much like his older brother, he's fallen victim to Cav's charms. I get it, trust me, I do, but Jase also has the complete picture in front of him. I didn't. Jase sees Cav as his savior, as some great messiah who saved him from humiliation and elevated him into legend status among the freshmen.

"Cavanaugh McLaughlin went to bat for him; he must be someone we need to know," they say. And Jase is lapping it up. He forgets about how Cav trashed my car, how he beat me up, how he's made my life miserable. He forgets who Cav pretended to be, the feelings he made me feel. He forgets I want Cav for myself.

His last words to me the other day haunt me. *You showed me what it could be like and I hate you for that.*

I have to admit that yes, I wanted him to remember what we had, wanted to let him know we could have it still, but I never realized how that vision could haunt him.

MEGAN LOWE

Despite everything, I want us to be together. Still. Even after this shit he's pulling with Jase.

I want to look at him and see him smile at me. I want to hold his hand and kiss him in public. I want to shout from the top of Sears Tower that this incredible guy is mine. But I can't.

I can't tell anyone how great he is, how he listens, *actually* listens when you pour your heart out to him. I can't tell anyone how his laugh hits me straight in my chest and hearing it, rare as it is, is the best thing ever. I can't tell how he gets me going with a single word and how powerful I feel doing the same to him. But what hurts the most is I can't tell *him* this. I can't go to him when I'm having a shit day, or when Amy says something that makes me steaming mad. I can't talk to him about cars and what I want to do to the Mustang. What's even worse is I can't tell Jase about it either. Not anymore.

"Where's Jase?" Amy asks as she comes in one evening.

"With friends," I tell her.

"Oh. Well, that's great."

"Yeah." I don't tell her how I wanted to stop him, *tried* to stop him.

"I know he's had a bit of a hard time finding his feet," she says.

"I think it's safe to say he's found them now."

"What about you?"

"Huh?"

"How are you finding things?"

I shrug. "Fine."

"Yeah? Making friends? Fitting in?"

I resist the urge to roll my eyes. "Yes, Aims, I'm making friends and fitting in."

She nods. "Good. I'm glad. And, um, what about boys?" she asks. "Anyone catch your eye?"

I arch an eyebrow.

She shrugs. "I'm trying to be supportive and, you know, involved in your lives."

I give her a smile. "No, there's no one who's caught my eye." And I don't think there will be. Cav, he... he's a pretty hard act to follow. So many nights I wake up, hard on raging, dreams of us together fading in my sleep-filled mind.

I don't think I've ever jacked off as much as I am now, not even when I first learned how good it felt when I was thirteen. I've tried taking the edge off by watching porn, but it's not the same. Apparently nothing gets me as hard as Cav does.

"Oh, well, there's no rush, right? You'll find someone when the time's right."

I nod. "Yeah, I suppose I will."

"So, um, what about you?" I ask. "Anyone special on the radar?"

She shakes her head. "No, no one special."

"I guess we're the perfect pair then, huh?"

"Who's the perfect pair?" Jase asks as he comes in, dumping his backpack on the stairs.

"Oh, just Connor, and me" Amy replies.

"Of course you are," Jase says. "The perfect two, and I'm the afterthought."

"Hey!" Amy says while I roll my eyes. "Connor and I

are far from perfect, and not once have you *ever* been an afterthought."

He scoffs.

"Don't worry about it, Aims," I tell her. "He's got his new friends; he doesn't want or need anything from us."

"At least my 'new friends,' as you call them, look out for me."

I shake my head. I've got to hand it to Cav, he works fast. But I guess fair is fair. I've "taken" and turned Thomas, so now he's "taken" and turned Jase.

"Jase," Amy gasps. "You know Connor has *always* looked out for you."

"Yeah, when it suited him."

I nod. "Yep, it suited me the entire time Mom and Dad were sick, but now they're dead, I guess I don't have to worry about you anymore. I should really thank them for doing me a massive favor."

"Connor...."

"I guess I should thank your new friends too for putting that thought in your mind. It's funny how you've never once accused me of not caring until right now."

Jase shrugs. "Maybe they opened my eyes."

"Or maybe they're blinding you with their lies."

"I think I'm finally seeing things clearly, actually," he says.

"Uh-huh, of course you are," I agree.

"Hey, you're the one who was telling me what a great guy Cav is."

"What a great guy *James* is," I correct. "It's clear they're two very different people."

"I have no idea what's going on," Amy says. No one stops to fill her in.

"They're the same person," Jase insists.

"Do you really think so?" I ask him. "Do you really think I could fall for someone like Cav?"

"I thought you said no one had caught your eye?" Amy asks.

"Who knows with you?" Jase says. "I know you're into some weird things, or have you forgotten we shared a bedroom wall basically our entire lives?"

I chuckle. "I see Cav's been working his magic on you," I say. "Tell me, has he admitted who he is yet, or is he still full of self-hate? You should tell him it's never going to go away, that it's a vicious cycle. Lust, hate, lust, giving in, hate. It'll just keep going and going, eating him alive."

"Are you talking about you or him?" Jase asks.

"I know who I am," I say, pushing my chair back and toppling it over in the process. "Can your new friend say the same? Can you, for that matter?" I ask as I storm from the room.

"So, that was interesting," Amy says, standing in the doorway of my room a little while later.

"Sorry about that. We've having some, um, growing pains, I guess."

She waves it off and comes and sits on the edge of my bed. "Siblings fight; it happens every now and then. I never thought it would happen between you two, but...."

"It happens," I finish for her.

She chuckles. "Yeah, it does."

"I was talking to a guy," I tell her. "Online. Things were going great, and I was trying to talk him into the possibility of more, and then poof, he ghosted me."

"It sucks."

"Yeah, it does," I agree. "His profile picture was a hand with a star-shaped scar. Long story short, this guy at school I'd been... arguing with has a star-shaped scar on his hand too."

"Cab and James," she says.

"Ca*v*," I correct. "But yeah. Let's just say he's even less receptive to me in real life than he was online."

"Oh. So how does Jase come into the story?"

"Cav's best friend is Thomas, who is now also my friend. He thinks I 'stole' him." I roll my eyes. "So he's using Jase to get back at me."

"Thomas Rose?" she asks.

I sit up. "How do you know his last name?"

She pats my knee. "Don't worry, I'm not monitoring you or anything. He's at the door."

CHAPTER 27

"Hey," I say, going downstairs and seeing Thomas waiting in the foyer.

"Hey, yourself," he replies.

"What are you doing here?"

He shrugs. "Would it be lame if I said I was in the neighborhood?"

"Is it the truth?"

"Well, yeah, but only after I drove here."

We both laugh.

"I um, wanted to see how you're doing, you know, with all this Cav and Jase stuff."

I blow out a breath and run my hand through my hair. "It's fucked up," I tell him.

He nods. "Yeah. I knew it would get messy, but I was hoping it wouldn't get *this* messy."

I shrug. "Cav knows what he's doing, I'll give him that."

"He does, but so do I."

I tilt my head.

"You ready to kick this shit off?"

"I don't know. Hasn't this already got out of hand enough?"

"I'd say it passed that a while ago. And I hate to be the one to tell you this, but I don't think it's going to get better any time soon."

I scrub my hands over my face. "This is so messed up."

He takes a step closer to me. "It is, but we can fix this. We *will* fix this."

I look up into his eyes. They're clear and determined. "Yeah, okay, let's do this." Honestly, Cav has me in knots. If it's not being horrible to me at school, it's his confusing words as James that keep coming back to haunt me. Then it's bringing my brother into our personal problems. For too long I've sat back and let him do all this to me. I've let him dictate our relationship but I think it's time I did something to change that.

"You want to grab a coffee or something? There's a Stan's Donuts a couple blocks away."

"Yeah, okay." I grab my jacket and yell to let Amy know I'll be back later. As I turn back to Thomas, I see Jase's head sticking out of his room. I ignore his narrow-eyed glare.

"Let's go."

W e grab a table in the small dining room, as well as a donut each and a coffee.

"I'm sorry Jase has been dragged into this mess," Thomas says.

I shrug. "You warned me against it. I warned him as well. He knew what could happen and he kept butting in.

I know he only wanted to protect me, but if he'd just left it, he would've been fine."

Thomas takes a sip of his coffee. "I'm not sure that's strictly true. I think Cav saw you starting to hit back at him, even if it is only slightly and he didn't like that. In Jase he found your weakness."

"Yeah." I play with the sugar canister, spinning it round and round. "I thought Jase was smarter than that, though," I tell him. "I thought he could see through what Cav was doing, coming in to play the savior. I didn't think he'd fall for it."

"Cav is the master at manipulation. Jase might be strong, but it would've taken a miracle for him to withstand Cav."

I blow out a breath.

"I just… I'm used to being the one Jase comes to when he has a problem. I'm the one who fixes them, who has fixed them for years now. And to hand that off to a guy who very clearly hates my guts? It's a hard pill to swallow."

Thomas nods. "I know. Cav does as well, which is why he's doing what he's doing. He *wants* to turn Jase against you."

"Yeah, well, it's working."

"And so will we."

"Well, well, well," a voice says as the bell over the door tinkles. "Isn't this cozy?"

I groan and drop my head to the top of the table.

Thomas grabs my hand, stroking the top of it. I try to pull away, but he holds onto me tighter. I lift my head.

"What are you doing here?" he asks.

"I was in the neighborhood," Cav replies. His eyes fall to Thomas and my hands. "What's this?"

I once again try to get out of Thomas's grip.

"Just two friends having coffee," Thomas says.

"Yeah, you guys are looking *very* friendly."

Thomas shrugs. "Connor's a great guy."

Cav scoffs. "Yeah, I bet he is."

"Wha—" I start, but don't get the chance to finish my sentence.

"You have a problem?" Thomas asks.

"Why would I have a problem? I just didn't think Connor here was your type."

"And if he is?"

Cav holds his hands up. "Then all power to you."

"Really?"

"Really," Cav confirms.

Thomas sits back, letting my hand go. "Interesting."

"Er, what's going on here?" I ask.

Cav shakes his head at me. "So this is how it's going to be, huh?"

"How what's going to be?" I ask. "I have no idea what's going on. Thomas and I are here having coffee and a donut, nothing more, nothing less."

"You keep telling yourself that."

"Why does it matter?" Thomas asks. "It's not like you're jealous, are you?"

Cav scoffs. "Just what do I have to be jealous about?"

"You tell me."

Cav nods. "So this is how it is, huh?"

"This is how it is," Thomas confirms.

"I don't know what you think you know…."

"Oh, I think I know *just* enough."

"You don't know shit," Cav says.

"Maybe I do, maybe I don't." Thomas leans forward. "But between us three, I think I know *exactly* what's going on. I think I know exactly what makes you tick, what gets you going." He looks over to me, still having no idea what the fuck is going on. "I think that I have finally figured you out and I'm going to make you pay for it."

"Is that so?"

Thomas shrugs.

"And you're confident about that? Willing to risk everything on it?"

"Confident enough. You think you have the whole world fooled," Thomas says. "You think you can say and do whatever you want and no one will question you. That ends now."

"And you?" Cav asks me.

"I-I just want to be left alone," I tell him.

He tilts his head. "Is that what you *really* want?"

I want to tell him that he knows what I really want. That *he's* what I really want, but I can't. I don't owe him anything but I can't spill his secret, I can't out him to his friend. I *won't*. So instead, I shrug.

"You messed with the wrong guy," Thomas says, picking up my hand again.

Cav shakes his head. "You really think this is going to work?" His hands are clenched by his side.

Thomas nods to them. "I'd say it's working *just* fine."

"You really have got me all figured out, haven't you?"

"Yeah, I think I have."

"And you don't have a problem with this, with him?" Cav asks me.

"Why would I have a problem?" I ask.

"Guess that's my answer then." He turns and walks out. He stops before he gets to the door. "I hope you two will be happy."

CHAPTER 28

"I'm so booooooooooooooooooooooooored," Chloe whines at lunch, a week after the Stan's incident.

Neither Thomas nor I have brought up what was said, both of us acting as if nothing happened.

"Why don't you have a party?" Thomas suggests. Things with Thomas are... a little weird, if I'm being honest. I don't know what he wants. I don't know what his endgame is and where he's going with it. I don't know why he did what he did and I'm too chickenshit to ask him about it. Then there's Cav, who despite everything, despite trying my hardest, I *still* can't get out of my head. Yes, I want him to leave me alone, to stop his bullying, but I also want him *want him*. And that's probably the most fucked up thing. How can I want someone who is so horrible to me? What does that say about me?

Chloe sits up. "A party?" she asks.

Thomas takes a sip of water. "Yeah, you know, where you invite people over to your house and there's drinking and dancing and more than a few couples will get it on in your bedrooms or a convenient dark corner."

She rolls her eyes. "I know what a party is."

"Then why'd you ask what it was?" I question.

"I didn't."

"Sure you did," I say, trying to hold my laughter in. It doesn't work.

"You guys suck," she says as we all laugh and throws a bottle cap at me.

"It was too easy," I tell her. "So what do you think?"

She tilts her head. "Yeah, okay. I suppose I could do a party."

Thomas and I smile at each other. I don't know where things are going with him, but I guess I have to play along. I've come this far and Jase is involved now. I guess if I want him to get out of this, I have to go along with whatever Thomas has planned.

"My house, Saturday night."

Chloe's house is insane. I've seen some incredible houses, but this has to take the cake.

"Holy shit," I say when I walk in.

"Right?" Thomas asks.

We wade through the flood of humanity, going through the front room, kitchen, basement, backyard, and pool house before eventually finding Chloe and some random girl in the indoor pool area. Even though the party is raging outside, we're the only ones who seem to have found this little oasis.

"Why do you have an indoor and outdoor pool?" I ask

Chloe when we find them.

She shrugs. "I don't know. Probably because of the sheer excess of it. The Fontana's always have to have the best, be the best. Apparently that means two pools."

"Huh," I reply.

"Come on in," she says, beckoning us into the water.

I look to Thomas, and we both shrug, stripping down to our boxers and getting in.

"This house is insane," I tell Chloe. Her lips are stuck to the other girl's neck, her hand inside her bikini top.

"Thanks. Here," she says, coming up for air. She pushes over a floating drink bucket. "Help yourself."

We spend the night laughing, talking, drinking, splashing, and generally having fun.

"I think I'm a little tipsy," the girl, who we haven't been introduced to, and obviously won't, says, finishing her wine cooler.

"Good," Chloe says, "I like it when you're looser."

With that, they're lost in a mess of tongues, and lips, hands wandering everywhere, eventually resulting in bikini tops being untied and bottoms sinking to the bottom of the pool. Thankfully, not that I get the feeling Chloe would care right now, we're still the only ones in here.

"I, ah, think we should take this down there," I tell Thomas, pointing to the other end of the pool as the moans increase from the girls.

"Er, yeah," he says, transfixed.

I laugh and grab him, dragging him to the opposite end.

"Here," I say, grabbing another beer and handing it

185

to him.

"Thanks." He twists the top of the bottle off and takes a long swig.

"Having fun?" I ask as I try to ignore the sounds the girls are making.

"Um, yeah," he says, eyes on what's happening down the other end.

"You can ask to join," I tell him. "I'm not entirely sure Chloe would be all that receptive, but if the other girl was into it, she'd go along with it."

He finally tears his eyes away. "Oh, um, no, that's okay."

"Are you sure?" I ask. "I don't mind. I'll even go and give you guys more privacy." Truth be told, I'm kind of hoping Thomas will go down there. We still haven't spoken about what happened at Stan's. There have been a few more touches usually when Cav's around, but I don't know what he's got planned or why he's doing what he's doing.

"No, that's okay, I'm good, really." He finishes his beer and takes another one.

"Are you sure? I don't mind."

He chuckles. "You trying to get rid of me?"

I shake my head. "N-No. I just thought that maybe you'd want to join in with them, they're probably more fun than I am."

He chuckles. "Oh, I think you're plenty fun."

"Is that why you're pretending to like me?" I ask. Clearly I've gained some liquid courage tonight.

"Who says I'm pretending?"

"Come on," I say. "It's okay if you do, I just... want to

know, you know, why."

"Is it not enough that you're a nice person and I like spending time with you?"

"Do you? Or are you only hanging out with me because of this thing you have with Cav."

"You have a thing with Cav, too."

I choke on the sip of beer I just took. How does he know what I have with Cav? Not that I have anything but...

"I-I don't have anything with Cav."

"So what would you call all the bullying he's done?" Thomas asks. He tilts his head back, draining this one as well.

"Oh, yeah." That. How could I forget? "I guess that's a... thing."

He laughs and moves closer to me. "Look, Connor, you're a great guy, and I really do enjoy spending time with you, my vendetta against Cav notwithstanding."

I shake my head and peel the label on my bottle of beer. This isn't happening. Thomas can't be falling for me. Can he?

He moves closer still. "You're a great guy, Connor, truly. You're a catch. Everyone who overlooks that is an idiot. Maybe *I've* been an idiot." He grabs a third beer and downs this one too.

My head snaps up. "What do you mean?"

He cups my cheek. "I think, maybe, I'm falling for you."

Blood rushes through my ears and I swear I'm about to pass out. "Y-You're not gay."

"Maybe I'm bi, or what do they call it? Pansexual? I fall in love with people regardless of gender."

"You're not in love with me," I rebut.

"Maybe not, but I could be."

I shake my head. "No, you couldn't." He can't be. There is no way this is happening.

"Why can't I?" he asks. "Because I used to like girls? Don't people have epiphanies like this all the time? Why can't I?"

"Because you're Thomas Rose."

"Uh-huh, and that means anything I want, I get." He presses closer to me. "I want *you*." He takes my face between his hands, his eyes zeroed in on my lips.

I feel like I'm having an out-of-body experience when his lips lightly brush mine, my hands frozen at my side.

Everything comes crashing down when the door smashes open, the sounds of the party filtering in.

Thomas kisses me once more before moving back. "Cav!" he says, arms outstretched. "You found us. Come join the *real* party."

"So he can turn me into a poof too?" he spits, nodding at me. "I'll pass."

Thomas raises an eyebrow. "For the right person, anything is possible."

"And *Connor*'s the right person?" he asks, jaw clenched, fists balled tight.

He shrugs. "Why can't he be? He's a great person. Funny, caring, a really great kisser. Seems like a catch to me. Anyone would be lucky to have him. Everyone should be fighting to have him. And now I've got him." His head lolls to the side.

"Thomas, I think you're drunk," I tell him.

He burps, the beer fumes overwhelming.

I grab his arm and drag him toward the steps. "A little help here?" I ask Cav.

Eventually he makes his way over and offers Thomas his hand. Thankfully, Thomas is a cooperative drunk, taking it and getting out without question.

I follow him and grab two towels from a stack, handing him one. "Here," I say as Cav helps him onto a deck chair where he promptly passes out.

I try not to breathe a sigh of relief.

"Really?" Cav asks, raising an eyebrow.

I hold my hands up. "I have no idea what that was. He just started saying all this stuff and then he... he kissed me."

"Isn't that what they all say?"

I shake my head. "You know I'm not interested in him."

"Maybe. Maybe not. If it's been a while, you might think any hole's a goal."

"Come off it, Cav," I snap, my liquid courage clearly still going. "I have been more than clear about what and whom I want."

"So have I," he rebuts.

"Why are you here, Cav?" I ask.

"Maybe I wanted a little social interaction."

"And you thought this would be the place for it?"

He shrugs. "Why not?"

I sigh and dry myself off. "What are you doing, Cav?" I ask.

"I should ask you the same question," he says. "Thomas?"

"I told you, I had nothing to do with that."

"Didn't see you putting up much of a fight."

"I was in shock! I don't know what he's doing either or *why* he's doing it."

Cav narrows his eyes. "You don't know why he's doing that, huh?" he asks. "You have no earthly idea?"

I shake my head. "No, I really don't."

"So you haven't been telling him stories?"

"About what?" I ask. "About you? Why would I do that? I haven't said anything this far, so why would I do it now?"

From the other end of the pool, the moans and screams increase. I grab Cav's forearm and drag him into a room, which, upon turning on the lights, is a bathroom. I shut and lock the door behind us.

"I'm not getting caught in here with you," he says, trying to get past me.

I put my hands on his solid chest and shove him. "For fuck's sake, Cav, just talk to me! You wanted social interaction, here's some social interaction."

"But I didn't want it with *you*," he says.

I throw my hands up. "Of course you didn't. You hate me. I get it. Sometimes the feeling is mutual. Why then, don't you leave me alone? You're the one who comes after me. Who slams me up against lockers, who beats me up in the cafeteria, who wrecks my fucking car. I have done *nothing* to you. But. You. Keep. Coming. Back. I want to know why, Cav. Why?"

He shuffles his feet.

I sigh. "Aren't you tired?" I ask. "Aren't you tired of hiding yourself? Pretending to be someone who you're not?"

"You don't know anything about me!" he yells.

"No?" I ask. "I bet I know some things your supposed BFF out there would *love* to know. He's using me to get to you, you know."

"Doesn't look like you have a problem with it."

Oh shit. I laugh. "Are you *jealous?*"

"What? No, of course I'm not."

"It's okay if you are. I'd be flattered, actually."

"You're delusional."

"And you're in denial. What a pair we make."

"There is no 'we' here."

I take a step closer to him. "There could be, if you wanted it."

"Of course I don't want it. Haven't you been listening to me?"

"I've been listening. Haven't you ever been told that those who protest the loudest have the most to hide?"

"I'm not hiding."

I'm close enough to cup his face, so I do. "Yes, baby, you are."

"Don't call me that," he pleads, his blue-gray eyes wide.

"I'll call you what I want," I say before taking his lips with mine. Almost immediately his mouth opens, his tongue battling with my own, but I quickly acquiesce, letting his tongue own mine. His arms come around my torso, pulling me to him, his body hard against my own.

"Shit," he pants. "You do taste like whisky and apple pie." He takes my mouth again.

I chuckle. "I thought I'd taste like beer and pretzels," I say as his mouth moves down my neck, nipping, and sucking.

"That too." He goes back to kissing me while I take the

opportunity to explore his body. I run my hand down his chest, undoing the buttons on his shirt as I do. We both manage to get it off, exposing a golden torso covered in ink.

"Wow," I say, taking a small step back to admire the works of art in front of me.

He shrugs. "You like what you see?"

I grab his hand and put it on my rock-hard cock. "What do you think?"

He drags me to him, his mouth owning mine once more, his hand dipping into my boxers.

"I've dreamed of getting my hands on this," he says against my lips, running his hand up and down my length.

"So have I." I fumble with his belt, eventually getting it undone, before lowering his fly, his impressive bulge pushing at the confines of his boxers.

I push his jeans and boxers down, his erection springing free.

"God, you're even bigger in real life," I mutter.

He laughs. "You say all the right things."

"I want you," I tell him.

He pulls back, and I freeze. Shit, did I take things too far? Is this the part where he cuts and runs?

His eyes sweep down my body, landing on my cock weeping precum. He licks his lips, and I swear to God, I almost lose it. Finally, he looks at me.

"You want me?" he asks.

I nod and swallow. "I do."

He looks to the side and grabs a towel. He throws it on the floor at my feet, before kneeling in front of me. "You can have me, but only after I have my fill of you."

CHAPTER 29

I swear my eyes roll back in my head when his mouth wraps around my dick.

"Oh, fuck," I hiss, my hands going to his head, the short strands of his hair tickling my palms.

"Mmm," he moans around me, the vibration going straight to my balls.

"Fuck, Cav, baby, that's so good."

He takes me deep so I hit the back of his throat, one of his hands rolling my balls around in his palm.

"Oh God," I moan, my head falling back and hitting the door.

A lot sooner than I'd like, I feel the tingling at the base of my spine.

"Baby, I'm gonna come," I tell him.

He sucks me deeper, his head bobbing faster, the hand that was playing with my balls moving to my ass. He stops for a second, sucking his finger before tracing my rim.

"Do it," I tell him.

He chuckles before pushing in.

MEGAN LOWE

I moan, but grab his head and direct it to my dick again.

He takes me deep, his finger working its way in and out of me.

It's not long before I empty myself down his throat.

My knees give out, and I end up on the floor next to him.

"Good?" he asks, a smile on his beautiful lips.

I bring them to mine.

"*So* good," I tell him once we break apart.

Once he determines I've obviously had enough time to recover he runs a hand up my thigh, over my abs and chest before coming back down to my rapidly hardening dick. "I liked that I could bring you to your knees."

I chuckle and run a hand through his hair. "You can do a fuckload of a lot more than that."

"Mmm."

"What about you?" I ask. "What can I do for you?"

"Anything you want."

"Anything?" I ask.

He nods, his eyes wide and clear, his face open.

I lean forward and kiss him once, twice, three times. "Can I fuck you?"

His eyes go wide. Despite that, he nods.

"You have a condom? Lube?" I ask. "My wallet's with my clothes." I don't want to tell him I have a feeling that if I open the door, the spell will be broken and he'll bolt.

"Y-yeah," he says, clearing his throat. "Over there."

I rifle through his pants and find his wallet, complete with a condom and two packets of lube. "Bingo," I say, holding them up, a grin on my face.

I lie back on my side next to him. "Have you done this before?" I ask.

He nods. "Once."

I kiss him. "We'll take it slow."

I open a packet of the lube and spread it over my finger. "Just relax for me," I tell him, pulling him to me so our cocks rub up against each other.

He moans and throws his head back.

I take the opening, kissing, licking, nipping, sucking while I trace his rim before slowly pushing in.

"Okay?" I ask.

He nods.

Slowly, I push in and pull out, and he gradually relaxes around me.

"That's it," I encourage against his neck. "You think you can take another?"

"Yeah," he pants.

I squeeze some more lube onto my fingers before gently easing them into him.

He grunts, but takes me in. "You good?"

"Feels good," he tells me.

"Wait until it's my cock inside you," I say before kissing him again. "We're going to be so good, baby, you'll see."

"Don't make promises you can't keep."

I lean back and cup his cheek. "This is one promise I am *determined* to keep."

He shakes his head, but I kiss him before he can say anything else. Now's not the time for that.

"Ready for another?" I ask when we break apart.

He nods. "Yeah, give it to me."

"I'll give it to you, all right," I tell him, once again lubing my fingers up.

"Fuck, yes," he moans when I ease my way in.

He pushes back on my hand, taking me deeper. I lie there for a moment, watching him, this guarded boy, not allowed to be his true self but so incredibly comfortable with me. I sweep my hand over his face and cup his cheek.

He opens his eyes.

"Hi," I tell him.

"I want you in me before I blow."

I chuckle but remove my fingers and slide on the condom. After another generous coating of lube, I position myself at his entrance.

"You ready?" I ask.

He rolls his eyes. "Just do it already."

His face morphs from impatience to a brief moment of pain, finally to bliss. He rests his head on my shoulder when I'm fully seated inside him.

"Feel good?" I ask.

He nods. "*So* good."

I pull out, then push back in again. "How about now?"

A moan is all I get in response.

I chuckle and press a kiss to his forehead as I move.

"Mmm," he moans. "That feels so good."

"Didn't I tell you?" I ask.

He chuckles and looks up at me. "Yeah, you did."

I flip us so he's on his back and I'm over him. "Never doubt me," I order.

"You're bossy during sex."

I lean down and give him a quick kiss. "I'm bossy when

it comes to you." I swivel my hips, and his eyes roll to the back of his head.

"Fuck, Con, I'm gonna…."

He reaches for his erection, but I smack his hand away.

"Mine," I tell him.

He whimpers, but I take pity on him, using the precum gathered at his tip to jack him in time with my thrusts. He's squeezing the life out of my dick, and I know it won't be long until—

"Fuuuuuuuuuuuuuuuuuuuuuuuuuuuuuuuuuuuuuuu-uuuuuuuuck," he moans as he comes all over my hand and our bodies.

The pure look of bliss on his face does me in, and I come, filling the condom.

"Holy fuck," I pant as I pull out of him, get rid of the rubber, and collapse on top of him. "That was incredible." I run my hand over his face again, never wanting to stop touching him. I place a soft kiss on his lips, and I know there's a goofy smile on my face that can only come from good sex.

"Don't give me that look," he says.

"What look?"

He pushes me off him. "The one that says 'finally.' There is no finally."

I sit up. "So this was…?"

"Nothing," he says, gathering his clothes and getting dressed.

"Bullshit."

He looks at me as he slides his boxer-briefs back on. "I told you we could never be anything."

"But that was before."

MEGAN LOWE

"Before what?" he asks. "Nothing's changed."

I get up and grab his arm. "*Everything's* changed."

"Just because you had your dick in my ass doesn't mean shit. The world out there," he points to the door, "hasn't magically changed since we've been in here."

"What about the world in here?" I ask. "Has that changed?"

He looks up from zipping up his jeans. "The world in here was never the problem."

"So we're just going to pretend like nothing's happened? Go back to hating each other?"

"I never hated you," he tells me.

I laugh.

He moves closer to me, then seems to think better of it and moves back. "Seriously, Connor, I *never* hated you."

I nod. "Uh-huh, *sure.*"

"It's the God's honest truth. I was afraid of you, afraid of what you made me feel, of what I would do to be with you. Afraid of what would happen when we did eventually give in to what's between us."

"Say I don't believe you."

He shrugs. "I can't make you believe anything you don't want to."

"Just like I can't make you believe that what we've got here is good?"

He nods as he does up his shirt. "Exactly."

"So nothing, none of this meant anything to you?"

He looks up, eyes blazing. "I *never* said that."

This time when he moves closer to me, he doesn't stop, pressing himself against me and cupping my face.

"This, what we have… *had*, meant everything to me, but I can't. We can't."

"You mean you won't."

He shrugs. "What's the difference?"

"Can't is someone preventing you. Won't is *you're* the one who's in the way."

"Either way, the outcome's the same."

I shake my head. "Fuck's sake, Cav. Why do this if you knew this wouldn't change anything? Why play with me, huh?"

"Because I couldn't help myself!" he yells. "I have watched you, wanted you for weeks, and it was killing me a little more each day. I want to be with you *so* badly, but there are other factors at work here, and I can't. Hate me if you want, but it's no more than I hate myself."

He leans forward to kiss me, but I push him away.

"You're a coward," I say, shaking my head.

He shrugs. "Maybe I am."

"Okay, say I accept what you're saying and we can't be together; does that mean I'm free to be with someone else?"

"I truly do hope you find someone to be with who deserves you."

"Because you sure as shit don't."

He nods.

"So you'd be okay if I went after, say, Thomas?" I ask. "He was pretty keen earlier tonight."

"I said someone who deserves you."

"And Thomas doesn't?"

"Thomas isn't who you think he is."

"You weren't either," I point out.

He chuckles. "Look how well that turned out."

"Who are you to decide if someone deserves to be with me or not?" I ask.

He steps closer to me, then again thinks better of it. "I'm just someone who wants the best for you."

I shake my head. "What if I've already found that? What if they don't want me?"

"Then they're not best for you. The person you're meant to be with will move heaven and earth just to get to you."

"Just go," I tell him, my shoulders slumping, back turned.

"I really am sorry," he tells me before unlocking the door and leaving me yet again.

CHAPTER 30

I don't know how long I sit on the floor of the bathroom. I don't know if the reason my eyes are shining is because of the tears that are welling or the fact I try to rub them away. At this point, I don't know anything.

Not wanting to put my wet boxer-briefs back on, I wrap a towel around my waist, angrily wiping away the evidence of Cav and my... whatever you want to call whatever the fuck just happened.

I wipe and I wipe, long past the time where there'd be anything left, leaving a nasty red mark on my abs.

I had him.

I had him, and now he's gone. Again.

I try to remember all that he said to me, but I can't find it in myself to care what he said. It doesn't mean shit anyway.

How can he experience what we just did and still not care? How can he walk away so easily from something this good? Because we could be; we proved tonight how good we could be together, and still he walks away? Who does that?

Someone who's scared, a voice in the back of my mind answers.

I want to tell him we're all scared, that living itself is scary, but I know it won't make a difference.

I take a deep breath. Despite what he said, Cavanaugh McLaughlin doesn't care for anyone but himself.

But yet, the little voice says again, *you can't stop thinking about him, wanting to be with him.*

I shake my head. I have to forget about him, forget about what happened here tonight, what happened months ago.

I open the door, the memory of Cav and me together disintegrating as the stench of chlorine floods in.

Thomas is still where we left him, passed out on the sunbed, golden skin gleaming. What was he playing at tonight? He can't be serious about being with me, can he? Or is this all part of his plan to get back at Cav? And if it is, why is he dating me going to work? Cav proved tonight that he doesn't want to be with me, and that's assuming of course, that Thomas knows he's gay, which I'm certain he doesn't. No one does. No one ever will. And that means he'll never be with me. But it's clear he didn't like seeing me with Thomas. Flashes of us together, visions of him on his knees before me, run through my head. I want him. I know this. I've always known this. And Thomas, perhaps inadvertently, is giving me a way to do that. Maybe. Possibly. Hopefully?

I run my hands through my hair and head over to my clothes. It's clear I'm not going to get anywhere tonight.

I slip my jeans on, commando, and pull on my shirt. Another glance back at Thomas shows him still peacefully asleep.

I grab another towel and cover him with it.

I take a side door out of the pool that leads me to the side of the house. I walk around the front and to my car without being seen, any effects of the beer long since gone. Chloe and her friend have obviously moved their party to somewhere more private.

I unlock the car and slide in, resting my head on the steering wheel.

What a night.

But, the little voice says, *what are you going to do now?*

CHAPTER 31

I did a lot of thinking over the weekend and came to the conclusion that I want to be with Cav. And that I think it's time I stopped being a little bitch and actually did something about that. I know what he said about not wanting to be with me, but I think that was his fear talking. I know he can't come out, at least not yet, but I'm willing to wait. I mean, I won't wait forever, but maybe if he knows I'm not going anywhere, that I'll be there for him like he was there for me with Amy, then he'll work on it. I see the way he looks at me. I know the connection we have. All these months he's been doing one thing, but telling me another. Well, I'm listening now.

Thomas is going to be a problem, but one I think I can use to my advantage. He seems to think the key to his revenge is by using me to get to Cav. So why can't I do the same? The groundwork is already set and it had good results on the weekend.

So I'm going to get my guy. No more good boy

Connor here. Sometimes you have to play hard to win hard. And I'm playing to win.

I start off like anyone does when they're trying to court someone. I figure out the code to his locker and put notes in there telling him I like his hair today, or that his essay in English was really great. Then I progress to candy, leaving chocolate bars, Butterfingers, of course, then Whoppers before a gigantic heart-shaped box of chocolates.

Then come the flowers, balloons, and stuffed animals. The look on his face when he opened his locker to find a massive Hello Kitty doll holding a heart was priceless. His friends all gave him shit, teasing him that obviously his latest piece didn't get his no-strings message. He waves them off, but his eyes inevitably find mine. Sometimes I see anger, or embarrassment. Other times I see annoyance. One time I think I saw humor, but only for a second. In the end, it doesn't matter what I see; it doesn't change anything.

"Holy shit," Thomas says as he sits down at our table in the cafeteria. "Did you see what Cav has in his locker this morning?"

I shake my head and feign ignorance. Today's present was particularly fun.

"It was full of extra large Trojans."

Chloe spits out her sip of water. "Seriously?"

Thomas nods. "Yup. I don't know who's doing all this, but it's funny as fuck."

Things with Thomas and me have been... normal. He hasn't taken our "relationship" further, but I think he's been occupied with what I'm doing to Cav to do anything in the meantime.

"Oh, man, that's gold," Chloe says. "I wonder what'll be next?"

"I don't know, but I wanna know. This shit is too good," Thomas crows.

Just then there's a chorus of wolf whistles as Cav, with Jase by his side, walks in.

Everyone gets to their feet, clapping and whistling. And Cav? Acts like nothing's going on.

"Well, that was anticlimactic," Chloe grumps as she sits back down.

"What did you expect?" I ask.

"I don't know, something. A bit of fun, maybe?"

"Because Cav is synonymous with fun," I deadpan.

She considers for a second. "Okay, point taken."

I watch as Jase and Cav get their food and take their seats, Jase folded in seamlessly as if Thomas was never there and Jase always was.

"Your brother's looking pretty cozy over there," Chloe says.

"Yup," I grit out.

I watch as Simon Brewer walks in, his group of Neanderthals with him, and doesn't even look in Jase's direction.

"But it looks like it's turning out for the better, though," she continues.

"That's Cav for ya," I say. "Savior of the friendless and bullied."

"It'll be okay," Thomas tells me. "Sooner or later Jase will realize what Cav's doing and will come back."

I huff, not so sure that's a possibility. "I just feel bad that he got dragged into all this."

"I think that he was always going to come into this, one way or another," Thomas says. "Whether that was defending you or as a pawn in Cav's game, the result was always going to be the same."

I grab the ends of my hair and pull. "I mean, I guess it's good that he's not being bullied at the moment, but…."

"You wanted to be the one to stop it," Chloe finishes for me.

I shrug. "Yeah."

Thomas touches my arm. "If you're worried about Cav…." He trails off.

I blow out a breath and run my hand through my hair. "He won't hurt him, will he?" I ask.

"No, I don't think so. Jase isn't his end goal. His end goal, for whatever reason he has, is you."

I nod. "Yup."

"I honestly think he's just using Jase to get to you, that's it."

"Okay."

He shuffles closer to me. "About Saturday night…."

"It's fine," I tell him. "You were drinking, I was drinking, let's forget about it."

"And if I don't want to forget about it?"

I blow out a breath. "Look, Thomas, I'm flattered by the attention but really, it's all good."

"That's just it, I don't think it is. You're a great guy, Connor. I've said that a heap of times and I've meant every single one. I want to get to know you better."

"Are you sure?" I ask. I know I was hoping this would

happen, but I want to make sure this happens in the right way. I don't want to push Thomas into anything he doesn't want to do.

He grabs my hand, threading his fingers through mine. "I am."

I nod. "Okay then."

CHAPTER 32

"What the fuck is going on here?" Chloe asks when she sees our hands.

"We're um...." I start.

"We're together," Thomas says, taking over for me.

"Since when?" she asks.

"Officially? Since now, but I think I speak for both of us when I say it's been building for a while."

She quirks an eyebrow at me. "Really?"

I shrug. "Yeah. I mean, it's no secret Thomas and I have been hanging out, but it um, progressed over the weekend." I realize that if I'm going to sell this to Cav, that I'm going to have to get more comfortable with being with Thomas.

I move closer to him and snuggle into his side. It takes him a second to realize what's going on, but when he does, he winds his arm around my back.

"So you're, like, gay now?" Chloe asks.

"I don't know about gay, but bi or pan or whatever you want to call it would probably fit better."

"And you're sure about this?" she asks me.

My eyes flick over to Cav. His jaw is clenched, eyes still narrowed. His gaze moves to our hands before coming back to my eyes. He then looks over at Thomas.

I feel a breath on my cheek before Thomas kisses me there, breaking the connection I have with Cav.

I look back to Chloe. "Yeah, I'm sure. We get along great and I'm excited to see where this goes."

"I think we're going to be great together," Thomas says.

For my sake, I hope we are. I'm crossing everything in the hopes that this ends how I hope it will.

My eyes find Cav's across the cafeteria. He jumps up from the table, the contents of his tray going everywhere, before stalking out of the room. He can say that he doesn't want to be with me, that I mean nothing to him, but his actions say different. I *know* he wants to be with me. I can feel it. And I don't think it's just me being hopeful. Cav and I have a connection. We proved that when he was James and we proved it again on Saturday night.

The news of Thomas and my coupling spreads fast, greatly aided, I suppose, by our—or more Thomas's—show at lunch.

We walk down the hall hand-in-hand, eyes following us everywhere we go.

"You okay?" Thomas whispers to me.

I nod. "Yeah. Are you?"

He chuckles. "Of course."

We stop when we get to my locker. His mouth is on

mine before I even really realize what's happening, his tongue tracing the seam of my lips. I let him in, the taste of pizza and Gatorade filling my mouth. It's a far cry from Cav's sweet and salty taste.

"Mmm." He licks his lips when he pulls back. "Is it weird that I'm *not* weirded out by that?" he asks.

I shrug. "I mean, no? I don't know. Do you want it to be weird?"

"No, I definitely don't." He kisses me again. "In fact, I kinda love that it's not."

"Love?" Cav scoffs, coming up to us. "You're in love with this fairy now?" he asks.

Thomas melts into my chest, his arm going around my shoulders. "So what if I am?"

Cav shakes his head, hands up. "Hey, all power to ya. My deepest congratulations. Where are you guys registered?"

"Come on, man," Thomas says. "Don't be a dick."

"But you like those now, don't you?"

"I like *Connor's,* you know, my boyfriend's," he specifies.

"Oh, is it special or something?"

I arch an eyebrow at him, which he studiously ignores.

"It's the person he is," Thomas says. "*That's* what makes him special."

"Holy shit, man, have you grown a vagina or something? You sound like a chick."

"Being man enough to own up to my feelings doesn't make me a chick, Cav. It makes me a man. You should try it sometime."

"I'm man enough as it is, thanks."

Thomas shrugs. "Whatever."

"Well, this is all very touching, but I've got better things to worry about than you two fags." He starts to walk away then stops, turning back to us. "You know, I thought you were better than this," he says before walking away again.

He doesn't say who he was talking to in particular, and neither of us ask, but I can't help feeling the sting of his words anyway.

CHAPTER 33

"You and Thomas, huh?" Jase says when he gets in the car that afternoon.

I shrug.

"How'd that happen?"

"The usual way, I guess."

"You guess?"

"Some stuff happened at Chloe's party and went from there."

"Do you like him?"

"Sure, he's a nice guy."

"You know that's not what I meant."

"We're going out; of course I like him."

"I heard he called you his boyfriend."

"So?"

"Just interested as to why you didn't use the same term?"

"Fine, he's my boyfriend. Happy now?"

"Are you?"

"What is this?" I ask. "Twenty fucking questions?"

"No, but it can be if you want it to be."

I sigh. "It just happened, all right? That's it; end of story."

He holds his hands up. "Okay."

"Thank you," I say, concentrating on the road.

"Cav is pissed, though."

My heart leaps. "Cav can suck it," I tell him. Until he comes to me, I have to be strong. What I'm doing is working, I just have to wait a little longer.

"He's a good guy, Con."

I sigh. "He might be, just not to me."

"Are you saying that because he rejected you?"

"I'm saying it because it's true."

"I think he's worried about you," he says.

Again, my heart leaps. But it's not enough. "He doesn't have a reason to be. I'm fine."

"And happy with Thomas."

"Yes! Fuck, how many times do I have to say it?"

Until you believe it, the voice inside my head replies.

"As many times as it takes to convince yourself it's true."

"Then I should've stopped after one. I don't need any convincing." I know I'm doing the right thing. My plan to play hard to get, to make him jealous is working. I just have to stay true and keep going.

"Yeah, keep telling yourself that," he mutters.

"And while you're at it, you can tell Cav to back the fuck off. What Thomas and I do is none of his concern."

"What if he wants it to be?"

"For what reason?" I ask. "To give me a hard time? To blame me for 'stealing' his best friend? Or so he can reject me yet again? He's made it more than clear he doesn't want me, and I've finally got the message and moved on."

"Have you though? Those condoms were pretty hard to miss."

"I don't know who that was, but it wasn't me."

"Come on, Connor. You can fool everyone else, but I'm your brother, I *know* you. Tell me, what's next?"

"Nothing's next. I told you, it's not me doing it. I've moved on, and if he's not happy with that, he knows how to change it."

"So you'd be open to a relationship with him if he came to you?"

"It doesn't matter, because that's never gonna happen. Plus, I'm with Thomas."

"Thomas is a distraction," he tells me. "Something to occupy you while you wait for Cav."

"I'm not waiting for Cav," I argue.

"Uh-huh, *sure*. Try that again, this time with feeling."

"He doesn't want me, Jase. For real. You can say he's pissed with Thomas and me for being together and that you think he's worried about me, but the fact of the matter is, he has had *many* opportunities to change things, and he doesn't want to. He's made it more than clear to me he doesn't want me, he doesn't want to be *with* me, so what am I supposed to do, huh? Sit around and wait for him on the off chance he decides he does? 'Cause that's bullshit, and I shouldn't have to do that. I should be free to be with someone who wants to be with me and isn't afraid."

"Have you ever actually taken the time to think about *why* he can't be with you?" he asks. "Have you ever stopped for one minute to think about how you've been rejected and wondered *why* he's doing it?"

"Because he's a coward."

He sighs and shakes his head. "It's not always so easy for everyone, Con."

"I'm not asking for a public declaration," I tell him. I glance over at him quickly. "Real talk?" I ask.

He nods.

"I like Cav, I do. A lot. Probably more than I should. When he was just James, I was happy to go along with whatever. He was there, I was here, and we met on an app, for Christ's sake. If things developed between us, then we'd take it as it came, and yes, I fell for him harder than I should, but he's also got to take responsibility for his part in all this."

"Has something happened recently?" he asks.

"Cav knows where I stand. If he wants to change things, the ball is in his court. But in the meantime, why shouldn't I be with someone who wants to be with me?"

"But Thomas? Really?"

I shrug.

"Is he even gay?"

"He says he's bi or pansexual."

"What the fu… fudge is pansexual?"

"It's where you fall in love regardless of gender."

"So he's basically bi."

"He's whatever he wants to be," I tell him.

"Don't you think this is like, *way* out of the blue?" he asks.

I shrug. I'm not going to tell him that this is all a part of Thomas's plan to being Cav down. He doesn't need to know that. And besides, maybe it's not all fake. Maybe he actually does have feelings for me. Stranger things have happened, right? "People fall in love at first sight all the time. This is way longer than that."

"*He's in love with you?*" he shrieks.

"Of course he's not. Calm down, for fuck's sake."

"Then why'd you say that?"

"As an example."

"*Do* you think he's in love with you?"

"Of course I don't."

"Do you think he's in this, you know, *for* you?"

"As opposed to what?" I ask.

"I mean, do you think he's in it *all the way?*"

"You mean is he ready for mutual blowjobs and taking it up the ass?"

"Well, yeah."

I blow out a breath. It's something I've been wondering myself. Just how far is Thomas willing to take this? How far am *I* willing to? "I don't know."

"Just stop this, Con," he says. "I can tell you don't like him like that, so why string him along?"

"I like him fine. I like spending time with him and we get along really well together. We have mutual goals and that's a good thing. I think we'll be great."

"Sounds like you're trying to convince yourself to be with him."

"No, I'm going to take it as it is and see where it goes, how it grows."

"But Cav—"

"Enough with Cav; I'm done with him. If he wants to change things, he knows where to find me." I pull up to our brownstone. "I know he's your friend or whatever, and I won't say shit about what I think about that. I'd appreciate it if you did the same for my relationship with Thomas."

He nods. "You're right. Cav is my friend, which is why I can tell you there's a lot more going on with him than you think. He does genuinely care about you and he worries about you, *but*"—he says before I can cut him off —"if you think you're doing what's best for you, then okay. I think otherwise, but I'll leave you to fuck up your own life." With that, he gets out of the car and goes into the house and straight to his room.

L ater that night, I get a text.
James: Be careful.

CHAPTER 34

"Hey, boyfriend," Thomas says to me the next morning before kissing me, his tongue slipping into my mouth.

He pulls back, a massive smile on his face, and brushes the hair back from my forehead, cupping my face. "I dreamed about you last night."

"Um, okay. That's nice," I say. While I'm glad Thomas is okay with what we're doing, I guess I didn't expect him to be so... enthusiastic about it.

He grabs my hand with his free one, threading our fingers together. "Yeah, it was a *very* good one."

"Oh, that's um, nice," I say again. I'm not sure how to act here. Yes, we're in a relationship, but it's not real. It's just for, you know, appearances, or whatever.

"I woke up hard as fuck," he says. "And it's all because of you." He tugs me to him, grabbing my ass, and devouring my mouth. I swear he's trying to taste what I had for breakfast with his kiss.

I push him away slightly. "Okay, let's just pull it back a little," I tell him.

He tilts his head. "Why?" He takes a step back. "Are you afraid to be seen with me? I thought we're boyfriends, that we're *partners*."

I put my hand on his shoulder. "We are, I just think we should pair it back a little, you know, not go too hard, too fast."

He nods. "Sorry. I just got carried away."

"It's fine," I reassure him. The truth is it's my own feelings that are fully preventing me from doing this whole way.

"So," he says, resting an arm above my head, the other pulling my hand to wrap about his back, "I think we got off to a good start yesterday. I think we definitely got Cav's attention."

I think back to the scene he made in the cafeteria. I nod. "Yeah, I think we did too."

"But we have to keep going," he says. "It's not enough to make him angry, we have to bring him down, destroy him, then set fire to the remains."

"Ah…."

"We're going to bring the great Cavanaugh McLaughlin down and it's going to be awesome."

"Are you all right?" I ask. I know Thomas is set on taking Cav down, I just didn't realize he was *this* invested in it.

He pulls back a bit. "Of course, why wouldn't I be?"

"It's just, you seem a little… different, this morning."

"It's a beautiful day and I have a beautiful boyfriend

who is helping me destroy my enemy, what's so bad about that?"

"Nothing," I say quickly. "It's just, you've never talked like this before. And not that I'm not glad that you're happy to be with me, but... well, you were straight up until the weekend."

He cups my cheek. "Maybe it took that long to see what was right in front of me."

"Um...."

He pulls back. "Are you sure this is what you want to do?" he asks. "I thought that we were on the same page, that we both wanted to take Cav down."

"I just wanted him to leave me alone. You're talking about something different all together."

He waves a hand. "Leave you alone, take him down, they both result in the same thing."

I shake my head. "No, they don't."

He takes another step back from me, his shoulders up, fists clenched. "Do you want to stop Cav or not?"

I take a small step closer to him, putting my hand on his chest. This side of Thomas is... well, it's frightening. "Hey, calm down."

He takes a breath.

"Good. Look, of course I want to stop Cav, but what you're talking about, the *way* you're talking about it? It's a little scary to me."

He blows out a breath and takes a step back. "Sorry, I just.... It's been a long time coming, that's all."

"Look, I get this is something you've been wanting for a while, but let's just take a breath and calm ourselves down, okay?"

He nods.

"Good. Like I said, I think we're on the right track here, but let's not push it, okay? We're good, things are going good, they're going to be good, let's just take that and see where it goes."

He nods again. "You're right." He blows out a breath. "I just... I want this so much, and being with you... it's like nothing else."

I chuckle. "Thanks."

He cups my cheek. "We're going to be great, Connor."

"Yes, we are."

The bell rings and he sighs. "I'll see you later," he says, giving me a kiss, before walking away.

Taking a seat in my homeroom, I blow out a breath. That was... unexpected. While I knew Thomas was committed to stopping Cav I guess I didn't realize just how badly he wants it to happen.

My phone buzzes in my pocket. I pull it out and find a text from Kevin.

Kevin: Meet Friday. You're up.

A message from Thomas comes in as someone sits down next to me.

Thomas: You get Kevin's text? You're up, baby, you're gonna do so good! XO.

"XO?" Cav asks, obviously reading over my shoulder.

"Jealous?" I ask, ignoring the fact he's not even in this class.

He nods. "You know I am."

I shake my head. "Don't tell me this shit, not when you can do something to change it."

"Can I though?"

"If you wanted to."

He shakes his head. "You make it sound so easy."

"It could be."

"No, it can't."

I sigh. "What do you want, Cav?" I ask. "As much as I love rehashing the same conversation over and over, it gets old."

"Did you get my text?"

I hold up my phone. "I get a lot of texts."

"Yeah, ending with a kiss and a hug."

I roll my eyes. "Yes, Cav, I got your text."

"And you're still with him."

"You're still not willing to be with me."

"Is that what it would take?" he asks. "Me to be with you for you to drop him?"

"Maybe. Or maybe I said that just to fuck with you."

"You can fuck me anytime," he says softly.

"Don't say that shit when you know it's not true," I snap. "I'm with Thomas. He seems really into me, which is a pleasant change."

He blows out a breath. "You like him?"

"Sure, he's a nice guy."

He nods and brushes a hand over his head. "You're racing on Friday?"

"Someone wanted me to prove myself," I remind him.

"That someone's an idiot."

"I know."

He gives a wry chuckle. "Just be careful, okay? With Thomas and the race."

"I will."

"Good." He taps the desk. "I'm sorry, you know, for everything."

"I appreciate that."

He gets up. "He's still not the guy you should be with though."

I shrug. "I can't be with the one I want. That's life, so you make the best of it."

He nods and is out the door.

CHAPTER 35

"**Y**ou ready for this?" Thomas asks as he massages my shoulders as we stand at the start line of tonight's race.

"Eh." I shrug.

He leans in closer, wrapping himself around me. "And when you win, we can celebrate." He bites my earlobe for good measure. He has toned down some, but every now and then has a tendency to get overexcited. I'm trying to go with it, keeping the bigger picture in mind, but it's a ride for sure.

I turn so I can see his face. "You sure you're ready for that?"

"Why wouldn't I be?" he asks.

"I dunno. It's a big step." One I honestly didn't think he'd be ready for, or prepared to take.

"But it's the next step in a relationship, so of course I'm ready for it. That's what you do when you're in a relationship, you show your love for each other, so that's what I'm going to do, I'm going to show you, and everyone else, that I'm in this, that I'm doing this, that I *can* do this, 'cause I can, and I will, and it's going to be fucking epic and I'm going to blow your mind and you'll never want to be with anyone else besides me." He says all this without taking a breath.

I reach and cup his cheek. "Hey, remember what we talked about?"

He nods.

"Just take a breath and calm down a little, for me."

He does as I ask.

"Good, that's good."

He shakes out the tension in his arms. "Okay, I'm good." He looks down at me. "I'm good about… being with you too."

"We don't have to. We can take things slow, I'm more than okay if that's what you want to do."

He shakes his head. "No. I need to. I *want* to."

"How about we just see how things go, huh? That way there's no pressure and if it happens, it happens. If not, then it's no big deal."

He grabs onto my hips. "Fine, but I *will* be having you tonight, or you having me, whichever way we do this."

I give him a smile. "We'll figure it out."

He leans down and gives me a chaste kiss. "Yes, we will."

I'm just about to say something, probably pushing my luck and disrupting the calm, when Jase walks over.

"Hey," he says.

"Hey. What are you doing here?" I ask. I rarely let Jase come when I race. He can't be in the car with me, not that I'd ever allow it, and I don't trust anyone else to look after him in case the meets gets busted up by the cops.

"Cav brought me."

"He *what?*" I ask, straightening and out of Thomas's hold.

Jase shrugs. "He brought me. He knows I wanted to watch you race, so we came."

"And did you tell him I don't let you come to meets when I'm racing?"

"Only because I don't have someone to 'look after me.' Well, I'll stay with him, so it won't be a problem."

"It's already a problem, Jase."

"Give the kid a break," Cav says, coming over to us. "You can't keep him locked at home like a prisoner or some shit."

"Better a prisoner at home than one stuck in juvie," I tell him.

Cav rolls his eyes. "So dramatic."

"Hey," I say, going over to him. "He's *my* kid brother, *my* responsibility. If something happens to him, that's on *me*."

"Chill, dude, I got him."

"Yeah?" I ask. "What else you got?"

"Hey," Thomas says, "It'll be fine."

I raise an eyebrow.

"I'll be right here with them, I promise. Two sets of eyes are better than one, right?"

"Anything even looks like it *might* be going south, you get him out of here," I tell him.

He smiles his soft, only-for-me smile. "I solemnly swear," he says before kissing me.

"If you two are done?" Cav says.

We break apart. "It'll be fine," Thomas says, taking my hand, threading his fingers through mine.

"Look after him," I plead.

He cups my face. "I will."

"You ready?" Kevin says, coming over to us.

I nod. "Yeah."

"It's a straight quarter-mile drag," he tells me. "First one to cross the finish line wins."

I nod. "And I'll be able to race next meet?"

"If you win."

"*When* I win," I correct.

He chuckles. "Just worry about the ten seconds it'll take you to finish first."

"I was aiming for nine, but ten will do," I tell him, casting another eye over my competition.

He claps me on the shoulder. "I'll see you at the finish line."

"Good luck, babe," Thomas says, coming over to me once Kevin has walked away.

"Thanks."

"I know you need to concentrate on the race, but don't forget about what's going to happen once you win."

I chuckle and give his hand a squeeze. He grabs me by the back of my neck, taking my lips with his, devouring my mouth.

"Just a preview for tonight," he says when we break apart, his hand sliding to my ass and giving it a squeeze.

"Come on, you fags," Cav calls. "We're waiting here."

"Watch Jase," I tell Thomas as I get in the car.

He nods, leaning in after me. "I will." He kisses me again and shuts the door.

Ahead of me is an empty stretch of road, probably about a mile or more, long, a thick yellow line painted 1320 feet from here.

I start the car and look across to the other two guys in the race with me. Their cars, a Honda and a Lexus, are impressive, but nothing can compare to the R-SPEC purring beneath me.

My phone, currently in the cup holder, buzzes.

Jase: Kill it bro!

James: Be careful.

A third message comes in before I put it down.

James: But good luck.

I look over at him; his face gives nothing away. I shake my head. This guy….

But at the moment, none of that matters. All that matters is the open road in front of me and the two cars beside me.

I have to give it to them, the Honda and the Lexus stayed with me… for a second. A *brief* second. But when the R-SPEC found her gear, that was it, end of story.

"Holy shit!" Thomas bounces around when he gets to me. "That was incredible, babe! I'm gonna do you so hard tonight."

I throw my head back and laugh, the adrenaline still coursing through my body.

"Seriously." He grabs my hand and puts it on his

crotch. "You made me *so* hard. I feel like I'm about to punch through these jeans."

I blush and laugh.

God, I'd almost forgotten what it was like to be in a race, to have nothing but the open road in front of you, a monster of a car beneath you, ready, and willing to respond to your every demand. It's a rush like nothing else and I missed it. The rush, it's almost enough to make me forget what Thomas said before the race and what he promises is going to happen now.

"Ahem."

We break apart to find Kevin watching. "That was some race," he says.

I shrug. "I told you."

He laughs as Cav and Jase come up, both of them with faces like thunder.

"Hey, guys!" I say, going over to them. "How good was that?"

"Yeah, woo," Jase replies, his voice flat.

"Oooookay, who pissed in your Cheerios?" I ask.

"No one. That was great, Con, really."

"Uh-huh." I turn to Cav. "And what do you have to say?"

He just shrugs, his fists clenched.

"All right then." I turn back to Kevin. "So does this mean I can race now?"

He nods. "You did good, kid."

"When's the next one?" I ask. I know the date probably hasn't been set, but I'm hooked. I want in.

He looks to Cav.

"I, ah, I'm not sure, I'll have to check."

"Have to check?"

"Yeah, see if there's a spot for you."

"You mean see if he'll allow me to race," I say, pointing to Cav, whom Kevin is still looking at. "I thought this was your organization."

"It is."

"But you're letting him dictate things?"

"It's his race."

"It's your organization," I hit back. "You said I can race, so I want to race."

"No," Cav says.

I throw my hands up. "What the fuck, dude? I did your little test, which I smoked by the way, and you're still denying me?"

"Come on, Cav," Kevin says. "You saw how he handled tonight. Think of the side action we'd get with you two going head-to-head."

I chuckle. "Of course you're getting a piece of the side action."

"Whatever, man," Cav says. "Race, don't race, see if I give a shit."

"Yes!" Thomas says, engulfing me in a hug from behind. "Man, are we gonna celebrate tonight!"

Cav clenches his fists tighter before stalking off.

"Dude," Jase says, shaking his head.

"I don't know what's the problem with you two," I tell him. "I won the race. Isn't that a good thing? I thought at the very least *you'd* be happy for me."

"I am," he insists.

"Uh-huh, 'cause the reaction I got at first screamed of you being happy."

"You know what my problem is," he tells me.

"And you know how I feel about that."

While we've been talking, Thomas has been getting increasingly handsy, kissing my neck, hands roaming all over my body. He's just slipped them under my T-shirt, rubbing my abs. "Can this family spat wait until tomorrow?" he asks.

Jase shakes his head. "Don't worry, I'm done here," he says before walking off.

"That was rude," I tell Thomas.

"So is keeping me waiting with this." He thrusts his boner into my back.

"A little waiting never killed anybody."

"Baaaaaaaaaaaaaaaaaaaaaaaaaaaaaaaaabe," he whines.

"Fine," I sigh. "Let's go."

"Best idea you've had all night." He kisses me quickly. "Meet you at mine. Don't make me wait any longer."

CHAPTER 36

Even though Thomas told me not to make him wait, I still offered to drive Jase home first. There was no way in hell I'd trust Cav to get him home safely.

As it turns out, Jase didn't want a bar of me. But that doesn't stop him bombarding me with texts as I make my way to Thomas's.

Jase: You're not seriously going home with him, are you?

Jase: He's a total douche, he doesn't even like you like that.

Jase: Cav is massively fuming. He doesn't want you with Thomas either.

Jase: Come on, Con. Be smart, think about what you're doing.

Jase: You could do so much better than Thomas, Con. Don't do this.

Jase: I know you don't like him like that either. Think about what you're doing.

Jase: Being with him won't make everything and everyone else go away, you know.

Jase: I know you're hurt, but don't stuff things up with Cav. Thomas isn't who you're meant to be with.

Jase: Thomas literally told us—

I don't read any more of his messages.

"Con, thank God," Jase sighs when he picks up the phone. "Are you on your way home?"

"You need to stop texting me," I tell him.

"Are you still at his house?" he asks.

"Of course I am. Where else would I be?"

"On your way home, which you should be."

"Thomas is my boyfriend," I remind him.

"Do you want him to be? Do you even like him like that? 'Cause I know he doesn't."

"He wouldn't be doing this if he didn't like me. This isn't something you can fake."

"Are you sure?" he asks. "How many girls have sucked your dick with you pretending they're Scott Eastwood or someone?"

"This is different," I insist.

"Is it?" He blows out a breath. "Look, Con, he told us some things tonight."

"How do I know that what you're saying is the truth?"

"What reason would I have to lie?" he asks. "*I've* never lied to you."

"Maybe not, but you're all up in Cav's business."

"He's my friend."

"He's using you," I tell him.

"Guess that makes us a perfect pair, 'cause Thomas sure as hell is using you."

I laugh. "For what reason? To get laid?"

"You don't even know," Jase says.

"I *do* know," I insist. "I know Cav's got his boxers in a bunch but won't man up and do anything. He hates that I've 'taken,' ha, Thomas from him and now we're dating."

"You're right, Cav does hate it, but so do I."

"He makes me happy," I reply.

"Does he? Really, truly happy?"

I don't answer.

"'Cause if he does, I'll back off, and I'll get Cav to back off as well. But, if he doesn't, if you're trying to convince yourself he does to get over whatever the hell you had or have with Cav, then this isn't the right thing to do, Con, and you know it."

Again, I'm silent.

"But whatever. Have a good night." With that, he ends the call.

"Hey! What took you so long?" Thomas asks when he answers the door.

"Sorry, I just rang Jase to check he got home all right."

Thomas takes my hand. "You're such a good brother. I love that about you." He pulls me inside, pushing me against the wall in the entryway and kissing the shit out of me.

He moans as he takes my mouth, grinding his hard-on against me, but I can't get Jase's words out of my mind.

Finally, he stops for air, his face shining as he looks at me. "How about we take this upstairs, huh?"

"Are you sure?" I ask. "Like totally and completely sure this is what you want to do?"

He cups my face. "I am totally and completely sure this is what I want to do, *you're* who I want to do, or to do me. Whatever works." He tilts his head. "Is everything all right?"

I shake my head to clear it. "Yeah, it's great. I just wanted to make sure you were sure. It's kind of a big step."

He presses closer to me. "But you'll look after me, right? Be gentle?"

"Yeah, of course."

"Then don't worry about me, okay? Tonight's about us, about taking our relationship to the next level."

"Going to the next level, yup." I nod.

"Are *you* all right?" he asks. "You have done this before, haven't you?"

I laugh, and even to me it sounds a bit on the hysterical side. "Of course I've done this before," I tell him. *In fact, just the other week I was inside your former BFF, and he rocked my world.*

I clear my throat. "And I'm fine. I guess the adrenaline wearing off is making me a bit loopy."

"Then let's get it pumping in a different way," he says, dragging me up the stairs.

Thomas's room is a typical teenage guy's room. Big bed, unmade, clothes all over the floor and his desk, a bookcase with a few photos and trophies on it, and a massive TV.

"I see you cleaned up for me," I joke.

He laughs and kicks some of the clothes on the floor into a pile in the corner. "Sorry."

"Guess you weren't very confident I'd win tonight, huh?"

He turns to me. "Of course I was."

And yet, he didn't bother cleaning up, even though he told me we'd end up here if I did.

"So, ah, what did you think of the race?" I ask. "You watched it with Cav and Jase, right?"

"Yeah, it was great."

"Did they think so? They were kind of... weird afterwards."

"To be honest, I have no idea what they thought. I was too focused on you to know what the hell was going on with anyone else."

"But if shit had hit the fan, you would've got Jase, though?"

"Oh yeah, hundred percent. Now, what are we doing standing here talking? There's a California King over there with our names on it." He nods to the bed.

"You have condoms and lube, right?" I ask.

He nods. "I should buy stock in Trojan," he jokes. "I buy so many of the suckers. Don't want any unwanted slip-ups, you know? Not, er, that that's a worry here."

I chuckle. "No, not a worry here. So, have you thought about how you want to do this?" I ask, stepping closer to him, herding him toward the bed.

"Um, not really?"

"Well, did you want to go all the way or maybe stop at

blowjobs, or not even go that far? Hand jobs work. Getting off is getting off."

"We can go all the way," he says.

I nod and push him on the bed, climbing on top of him. "Okay," I say as I kiss his neck. "Do you want to bottom or top?"

"What do you usually do?" he asks.

"Depends on who I'm with and what they want. I'm good with either."

He thinks for a minute. "I think I want to do you, that's what a man would do, right?"

"Er…" I have no idea what to say to this, or why I'm even here in the first place. I don't know what Thomas is doing either. We don't have to do this, but for some reason he's got it in his head that he has to. "You know we don't have to do this, right?" I say, reminding him one more time.

He nods. "Yeah, but this is what relationships are about. Besides, if we want to be legit, then this is what we have to do."

"If we want to be legit… Thomas, what are you on about?"

He looks to me. "We have to prove that we're a real couple."

"How are we *not* one? And what makes one real or not real? We kiss, we hold hands, we hang out together, that's real, isn't it?"

He comes closer to me, his hands on my hips. "Of course it is, babe, but eventually relationships go past that, they get to the good stuff. Don't you want to the good stuff?"

I sigh.

He starts kissing my neck, his hands running under my shirt, rubbing my back, my abs. "Come on," he says. "You want this, I know you do."

He pulls my shirt off, then starts kneading my butt. I know I should stop him, that this isn't right, that this isn't the right thing to do, but his hands feel so good.

He smiles against my neck as I run my hands up his arms. "That's it, baby. We're so good together aren't we? We're gonna show everyone how good we are."

"Mmm."

He undoes my pants, dropping them to the floor. "I've been dying to get my hands on this," he says, as he slips his hand into my boxer-briefs, pumping me slowly. I begin to harden in his hand. "Yeah, there we go."

"Shit," I curse.

"Am I doing it right?" he asks.

I nod. "Y-Yeah."

He lifts his head and smiles at me. "Fuck, yeah."

He starts to pump me harder, faster.

My hips start moving of their own accord, fucking his fist.

"Yeah, that's it."

"Shit, I'm gonna come," I say.

"Do it," he tells me.

"Fuuuuuuuuuuuuuck." I come all over his hand.

"That was awesome," he says.

"Glad you found it as enjoyable as I did," I tell him as I take my boxer-briefs off and use them to clean myself up a bit.

He grabs the back of my neck and pulls me into one of his forceful kisses. "Now *that* was real."

"I think it's your turn now." I mean, it only seems fair. I got off, so should he.

His eyes light up and he strips out of his clothes in lightning speed before hopping on the bed, his erection lying flat against his stomach.

"You ready for this?" I ask, getting on the bed next to him.

He nods. "*So* ready."

I lower my head, taking him in my mouth.

"Oooooooooooh," he moans as I take him to the back of my throat. "That feels *good*."

I hit all the sweet spots, his crown, and the spot underneath.

"Fuck, that's it," he says.

I let him go with a *pop*. "You want to come in my mouth or you want to do this?" I ask.

"We said we'd take it all the way, so we should take it all the way."

"We said we'd see how things go," I remind him. "If you're not ready or not comfortable we can just leave it at bjs and call it a night."

He shakes his head. "No, I can do this. I want to prove to everyone that I've got what it takes, that I can do this. I can and will." He grabs my face. "We're doing this."

"It's okay—"

"*I said we're doing this*," he grits out.

"Okay," I agree.

I reach over and grab the lube. "Give me your finger," I tell him.

"What for?" he asks.

I grab his hand and point his index finger, squirting lube on it. "You have to stretch me so I can take you." If he wants to do this, we're going to do this. And maybe, just maybe, I'm calling his bluff.

"I have to… *stretch* you?"

"Yeah. Don't you have to work girls up the same way?"

"Ah, I dunno. I usually just shove it in."

Well, that sounds delightful. Those poor girls. "It's called foreplay, babe. Here." I take his hand and position it at my ass. "Run your finger around my rim, lube me up good, and then slip your finger in. After a while we'll add a second, then a third. Then you can have me." I place a chaste kiss on his lips.

"Umm, okay."

Slowly he traces my rim before pushing his finger inside me.

"That's it," I encourage.

"This is like, hygienic, right?" he asks.

"As hygienic as me sucking your dick a minute ago."

He nods. "Okay, it's okay."

I pull back a little. "Do you want to stop?"

"What? No, no, this is fine, just, you know, a little weird."

I cup his face. "This is real, baby. That's what you wanted, right?" It's clear to me that for whatever reason, Thomas is determined to go ahead with this. The only way I'm going to get him to stop, or at least think about what we're doing, is to throw him in the deep end.

He nods. "Right."

I lean in and kiss him again. "I know it didn't sound

243

like it before, but I really do want to take our relationship to the next level. You're such an incredible guy, and I'm so fucking lucky I have you."

"Um, yeah me too," he says.

"We're great together, aren't we?"

He nods. "Yeah. Can we get back to the, um, good stuff now?"

I grab his dick and begin to stroke it. "Like this?"

"Yeah, but more."

"You want more?" I ask.

"Yeah, yeah, I want all of it."

"Are you sure? Like *really* sure?"

"Um...."

"'Cause, baby, it's a lot."

He shakes his head. "I can take it. I can take it. I *can*."

I sigh. "All right, babe. Let's do this."

CHAPTER 37

C av is waiting for me inside the school doors on Monday morning.

"Have a nice weekend?" he asks.

"Yeah, we did. Thanks for asking."

He scoffs. "We."

"Yeah, me and Thomas. You know, my boyfriend, your former best friend."

"He's still my best friend."

"Is he?" I ask. "Have you checked with him lately?"

"I don't need to check."

"If you say so. I've been told you guys weren't getting along on Friday night, but maybe I heard wrong."

He drags me to an empty classroom, locking the door behind us and slamming me up against the wall.

"You know what he said to me and your brother on Friday night and you still went home with him?"

"It doesn't matter what he said, it matters what he did. He's not afraid to show me he wants to be with me. He's not afraid to be with me period. *That's* what matters to me."

He shakes his head. "So it doesn't matter what he believes or why he's with you. As long as he keeps *showing* you he wants to be with you, you don't care about the rest?"

I shrug. "I want someone who wants to be with me. I'm not going to apologize for being with someone who also wants that."

"What if I want to be with you?" he asks, crowding me, resting his arm next to my head. "What then, huh?"

I've waited so long to hear these words from Cav's mouth, but why is he saying them now? Is it because of what he thinks Thomas and I got up to on the weekend? Or is it because he genuinely wants to be with me? Because he's ready?

"Do you really want me?" I ask. "Or do you only want me because you can't have me? Because Thomas has me?" This is what I've hoped for, but it's not enough. Jealousy is not going to be enough. It has to come from the heart and right now Cav isn't thinking with his heart.

"Thomas doesn't want you, not like *I* do." He cups my face.

"He's with me now, and not because someone else has me."

"Is he really? Do you even know why he's with you? Did Jase tell you exactly what he was saying?"

"I don't want to know, and I don't care. I told you before, Cav, his actions speak louder than your words."

"They're not mine, they're his."

I sigh. "It doesn't matter. He was there for me, is here *with* me. He stayed after as well."

"After?" he asks. "Oh." He steps back when he figures it out. Not that Thomas and I ended up having sex on Saturday, but Cav doesn't need to know that.

"Thomas and I have a good thing going, a *really* good thing. Why should I ruin that for someone who isn't even sure they want to be with me?"

"I *do* want to be with you." I have waited so long for Cav to tell me these words, but can I trust them? Can I trust him?

"Will you hold my hand as we walk down the hall?" I ask. "Kiss me in public? Sit with me at lunch? Make one of those cute couple TikToks? I get it, your family sucks and you're not out, but I am. And yeah, my parents were understanding, so I don't get what it's like for you, but...." I shake my head. I look up into his beautiful blue-gray eyes. "I like you, more than I should. And I do like you, I do want to be with you, not just in private, but in public as well. I *want* to hold your hand in the hall and kiss you in public. I want to show you off and show everyone how fucking lucky I am that you're with me, that you chose me. I also.... I also want you to be proud to be with me, to be seen with me, to kiss me, to love me." I close the distance between us. "This, what we have between us, it isn't wrong, Cav. It's not a sin or unnatural or whatever the fuck you've been told it is. It's just love, baby."

It's his turn to shake his head.

"Yes, it is," I insist. "When I kiss you, does it feel wrong?" I brush my lips against his. He moans and chases me when I pull away.

MEGAN LOWE

He grabs the back of my neck, holding me in place and resting his forehead on mine. "No, it doesn't feel wrong."

"When we were together the other week, did it feel wrong?"

A tear slips down his cheek. "No, it didn't."

"How did it feel?" I ask.

Another tear falls. "It felt right," he says. "It felt like I was home, that the piece I've been looking for finally slotted into place. I felt… at peace."

I nod. "Imagine how it would feel to be like that all the time."

He sighs.

"You can do this. *We* can do this. We can be together."

"My mom—"

"We'll deal with her. But baby, you need to do something. You can't keep living your life in the dark. It's not fair to you or healthy. You can't keep this bottled up."

"You're with Thomas," he says.

"Say the word, and I'll end it," I tell him. "Tell me you want to be with me, you want us to be together, to be a real couple, out and proud, and I swear I'll end it this very second." I pull my phone out of my pocket. "In fact, I'll call him right now." I scroll through my contacts until I get to his name, pulling up his information. I don't want to call his bluff, but I have to know if he's in it for real.

"Wait," Cav says, covering my hand.

I sigh and put away my phone. "I can't go back into the closet, Cav. I won't be someone's dirty little secret."

He runs his hands through his hair. "Why not?" he asks. "You were fine with it when we were just talking. Why can't we go back to that?"

248

"Because I fell in love with you," I say. "Or as close to it as I could. I didn't mean to, and I know you warned me, but then you turned out to be you and I couldn't help it. All the games we've been playing? The blatant jealousy oozing out of you? There's a reason for that. Feeling what I do? That shouldn't be hidden, and you shouldn't ask me to."

"Fuck!" he yells, grabbing a desk and flipping it over. "Why are you doing this to me?" he asks, his eyes wide, mouth tight. "I was fine before I met you. I had what I needed, and everything was simple and easy."

"It was easy because it didn't mean anything. The important stuff, the stuff that's going to mean the most? You have to fight for it so you can appreciate what it took to get it."

"I didn't ask for any of this."

"If that was true, you never would've swiped on my profile."

"Maybe that was a mistake."

"Was it?" I ask.

He shakes his head. "No, it wasn't."

Once again, I close the distance between us and cup his face. I love the feel of his stubble on my palms. I will never touch him enough, every time wondering if it's the last time. "You can say you want easy, but it can be. Baby, all of this can be ours if you just say the word." I lean up to his lips. "Say the word, Cav."

He pulls away, storming to the door and tearing it open, people scattering as he walks away from me yet again.

CHAPTER 38

"Hey, babe," Thomas says, kissing me when I sit down at our table in the cafeteria.

"Hey," I mumble.

"What's wrong?" he asks, wrapping an arm around me.

I wave him off. "It's nothing, I'm good." But I'm not. Cav's and my conversation is swirling in my head. He wants to be with me. He *wants* to be with *me*. And I want to be with him. This is what I've wanted, why I started all this nonsense with Thomas, but Cav's not ready. I know he's not. It doesn't mean that my heart isn't telling me to fuck it all and take the chance.

"Yeah?"

"Yeah," I confirm.

He tilts his head. "Yeah, I don't think so. I know you better than that; something's eating you."

I shake my head. "I'm fine, really."

He folds his arms across his chest. "I don't believe you."

I crack a smile. "It's fine, really."

"If you're sure…."

I give him a chaste kiss. "I'm sure, but thank you. I appreciate the offer."

Someone scoffs as they walk past. I look up to find my brother.

"Jase, hey," I say.

He stops but doesn't look at me. He ignored me all weekend too, not answering my texts or talking to me when I got home yesterday afternoon. "Hey."

"Are you going to look at me?" I ask.

He turns his head, eyes flat, jaw clenched. "Better?"

"Not really."

"What do you want, Con? My friends are waiting for me."

Thomas chuckles. "Cav isn't your friend, dude. He's using you to fuck with Connor."

"Just like he used you for all his dirty work, right?" Jase hits back.

Thomas sits up straighter. "I came to my senses."

Jase laughs. "Is that what it's called?"

I ignore their bickering. "How's your day going?" I ask.

"Why d'you care?"

I rear back. "Are you serious?"

"Are *you*?"

"What's that supposed to mean?"

"It means you're still with this dick even though… people are telling you to wake the hell up."

"Dude, what's with the hostility?" Thomas asks. "I'm a good guy when you get to know me."

"Are you?" Jase retorts. "You told my brother the real reason you're with him?"

Thomas turns to me. "Okay, I have to confess the real reason I'm with you."

"And what's that?" I ask, my heart almost pounding out of my chest.

His hand slips down to my ass. "This incredible ass. I can't get enough of it."

He bursts into laughter. Chloe is frowning, and Jase shakes his head.

"Oh, come on, little Siddell," Thomas says. "That was funny! I honestly don't know what you and my former best friend have against me, but there is absolutely no sinister motive to my wanting to be with Connor."

"Why are you doing this?" I ask Jase.

"You know why," he tells me, eyes darting back to Cav.

"And I told you, it's not going to happen."

"What if it could?"

"It can't, so drop it."

"Come on, Connor, don't give up now."

I get to my feet. "I didn't give up on anything. I have tried and tried and got nothing. Why should I be the only one who gives something up, huh? Isn't it enough I practically gave up the past five years to help Mom and Dad? Why can't I have one thing for myself? Haven't I earned it? Don't I deserve it?"

"Some things you have to fight for so when you have them, you appreciate them," he says, throwing my words from this morning with Cav back at me.

I stagger against the table. "I have fought," I choke out. "But it can't be one-sided."

"Maybe it's not. Maybe you just can't see the fighting on the other side." With that, he walks off.

Thomas rubs my back as I sit back down. "You okay?"

I nod. "Yeah, I'm fine."

"I don't know what your brother's problem is, but don't listen to him, okay? Cav just wants to get back at you because we're close now. He'll say and do anything to fuck up our happiness."

I nod again. "You're probably right."

He flashes me his boxer-melting smile. "So we're good?"

I lean forward and kiss him. "Yeah, we're good."

CHAPTER 39

I know the fierce winds that whip off Lake Michigan aren't why they call Chicago the Windy City, but it's one hell of a coincidence. The gale is freezing, I can practically see icicles floating around me, but still I sit here, freezing my balls off.

How did I get here? I never wanted to be the guy who forces someone to do something they can't or aren't ready for. Especially when that something is coming out. I shouldn't be forcing Cav. I know I should be patient and understanding and help him through it, but would he even want that? Maybe I should just do it anyway.

And Thomas…. How the fuck did things with him end up as they are? This all started as a way to stop Cav bullying me but it's morphed into so much more. And some of the things Thomas has said…. Some of the things he's done…. They're downright worrying. But how can I get out of this arrangement without making things worse?

I just don't know.

I scrub my hands over my face.

Every interaction I've had with Cav/James flashes through my mind.

I'm falling in love with him. Hell, I may have already fallen, for all I know.

If I'm honest, I know it's him I want to be with. I want to hold his hand as we walk down the hall at school. I want to kiss him when I win at the Skids. I want to take him to eat pancakes at Wildberry.

Does he want the same? I think he does, but he won't do anything so we can. Is it fair for him to ask me to wait? For how long? A year? Two? Ten? I want a life with someone. Perhaps that person is Cav; I don't know. I'd certainly like to find out, though.

I want someone to grow old with, who lights up when I walk through the door. I want someone who wants kids with me. I want someone to tease me when I freak out when I find my first gray hair.

I think Cav wants that too.

I never thought I'd find someone I truly wanted to be with on a hook-up app, but yet, here we are. I know it sounds crazy. I'm eighteen and forever is a long time, but I can see it. Or maybe that's my romantic brain taking over again.

And then there's Thomas. I don't know what he's playing at, what he's trying to convince himself of. He's not bi or pan. He's definitely not gay. He's just... lost I think. He has this hatred for Cav and he's willing to let it take over his life. But he doesn't love me anymore than I love the Bears. He is one master planner though. His plan to get back at Cav worked a treat.

But did it work the way I hoped it would? Does Cav want to be with me or has his jealousy driven him to say all those things to me? Does it really matter? If he wants to be with me, he wants to be with me, right?

Cav is kind, and thoughtful, and considerate—in private. When I was going through all that shit with Amy, he listened, actually listened to what I had to say and helped me work through it. How can I ignore that?

How can I turn my back on someone like that?

Cav has his own path to travel; so do I. Will our paths converge? Will we get our shit together? Will *he* get his shit together?

I can't imagine what he's going through. My parents were great when I came out, so this whole thing is new to me. One thing I do know, though? That no one, regardless of who they are, should have to live their life hiding away. That means Cav living in the closet and me right along with him, if things go that way.

And I meant what I said when I told him I'd drop Thomas. I just have to figure out a way to do that that doesn't risk angering Thomas further.

Maybe I just should end things with Thomas regardless. What we have, it's not healthy. For either of us. He needs to move on from whatever it is he has against Cav, and I, well, I need to figure out if what Cav is offering is sincere and will be enough for me.

"Fuck!" I yell, scaring an older couple walking past. I hold my hand up in apology.

"Scaring the elderly a new hobby of yours, is it?" Chloe says as she sits down next to me.

"What are you doing here?" I ask.

She shrugs. "Thought you might need someone to talk to. Although we can just yell at people if you want."

I nudge her. "Funny."

"I know. So, you going to spill or what?"

I blow out a breath. It clouds the air in front of us. "I think I've fucked up."

"Oh, there's no thinking about it. You definitely have."

"Gee, thanks for the vote of confidence."

"I'm your best friend. I don't give you confidence; I give you the truth."

"And what's that?"

"That you've fucked up."

I chuckle. "Thanks."

"You know what you've done," she tells me.

I nod. "Yeah."

"And you know what you have to do."

"So why can't I do it?"

She shrugs. "I dunno, maybe because you're a pussy."

"I thought you like pussy."

"Good pussy, not a weak one."

"Are you saying I'm weak?"

"Why are you with Thomas, Con?"

"Okay, point made."

"I know you're only with him to make Cav jealous."

"H-How do you know that?" I ask.

"If you know where to look, you can see it written all over both of your faces."

I scrub my hand over my face. "Fuck."

"Look, I know things aren't going to be easy with him, not by any stretch of the imagination, but surely difficult with him is ten times better than great with Thomas. Ugh, even thinking about you with him…." She shudders.

I nudge her again.

"What the fuck were you thinking with him?"

"I was thinking that it would be fun to make him jealous."

"And how's that working out for you?"

"Well, I think he's jealous…."

"I'd say that's right."

"But maybe it's not as fun as I thought it would be, and that Thomas is going to be a bigger problem than I ever thought he would be."

"He's a problem, all right."

"Fuck, this is so fucked-up."

"Yup."

"I'm going to have to be the one to make the move, aren't I?" I ask.

She nods. "Yup."

"Thomas isn't going to let go easily, will he?"

"Nope."

"Fuck me."

"See? That's where you went wrong. You were thinking with your dick."

"I happen to like my dick."

"And look where it's got you."

In a big fucking mess, that's where.

CHAPTER 40

The following day I find a rose, exactly the same as the bunch I sent Cav, in my locker.

"Someone's sending you flowers?" Thomas asks. "Should I be jealous?"

I quickly shut my locker. "I'm sure they put it there by mistake," I say.

He slings an arm around my neck. "You know, if you wanted flowers and candy and all that girly shit, all you had to do was tell me. You didn't have to send it to yourself."

"Ha." I know my response leaves a lot to be desired, but my head is spinning even more than it was before. What does the rose mean? Is it from Cav? I'm pretty confident in assuming it is, but maybe it's not. If it is from Cav, is it a good thing or a bad one? Why couldn't he leave a note?

I look for him in the hall but can't find him anywhere.

"Who are you looking for?" Thomas asks, breaking into the fog around me.

"Huh? Oh, no one. Just trying to work out who sent me the rose, that's all."

"And what? You think they'll have a neon sign on, pointing and telling you it was them?"

"You never know."

He laughs. "Who the hell sends a rose anyway?"

"Some people think it's romantic. Why? What would you send?"

"I wouldn't send shit. You just go up to 'em, grab their ass, and lay one on 'em."

"What if they don't want that?" I ask.

He scoffs. "Who wouldn't want me? I'm the motherfucking catch of this goddamn school."

"And modest too," I say.

He shrugs. "If it's the truth, why hide it?"

"Who says it's the truth?"

"Oh man, if only you knew the amount of pussy I turn down on the regular."

I shake my head. I know a normal boyfriend would be upset with a comment like that, but let's face it, I was never a "normal" boyfriend to Thomas. And he was never one to me.

"Sorry," he says. "I shouldn't have said that. That wasn't right."

I shrug. "It's fine."

He pulls me to a stop. "No, it wasn't. That wasn't a very nice boyfriend thing to say."

"I think we both know that this isn't a typical relationship."

He tilts his head. "What does that mean?"

"Thomas—"

"No, wait!" he says. "I know I haven't been the best boyfriend lately, I've been up and down and all around, but I'm trying, I really am."

"It's fine," I say.

"No, it's not. I want to be with you. You're the first person who's ever really understood me, who's taken the time to get to know me. I don't want to lose that."

My shoulders drop.

"And I know I need to do better. I *will* do better." He cups my cheek. "You'll give me another chance, won't you?"

"I-I...." I look up, straight at Cav.

He clenches his fists, shakes his head, and turns and walks away in the opposite direction. The tightness in my chest tells me what I don't want to admit.

"Thank you, baby," Thomas says, clutching me to his chest. "I promise I won't let you down."

Try as I might, I can't get the rose and the look on Cav's face as he walked away out of my mind. I try to catch him in the hall between classes, but he slips between my fingers, disappearing in the crowd before I can get a word out. Then there's the look on Thomas's face when he convinced himself I would give him another chance. He's been on cloud nine ever since. It doesn't make me feel any better though.

It's still bothering me when I sit down for lunch, twirling my fettuccine alfredo around my fork.

"There's my awesome boyfriend," he says, setting his tray down and pressing right up against me.

I shuffle down.

"What's the matter?" he asks.

"Nothing," I say. "Just wanted to give myself some room to move, that's all."

"Are you sure everything's okay? This doesn't have to do with the rose and what I said this morning, does it?"

"What if I said everything wasn't okay?" I ask.

"Then I'd say I'm super fucking worried about you and would want to know what I can do to make it better. That's what I'm here for after all, isn't it? To make your life better?" He snuggles into my arm. "Because you sure as fuck make mine better."

I sigh. Why did he have to say that? How the fuck am I supposed to break up with him when he says stuff like that?

"It's nothing. I'm just thinking about Jase, and I'm pretty sure I just bombed Mr. Skaff's pop quiz in chemistry."

"Aww, babe." He rubs my back. "You're such a good brother, and I'm sure you did fine on the quiz."

I shrug.

He moves closer, his other hand moving up my thigh to cup my dick. "I can make it better. You know, take your mind off everything if you want?"

"It's fine."

"No, it's not. I know what you need and I'm going to give it to you." With a grin, Thomas gets up, grabs my hand, and drags me out of the cafeteria. A chorus of wolf whistles follows us.

We come to a closet, which he opens, flicks on the light, and pushes me in.

He follows, shutting the door behind him.

In a flash, he's all over me, pushing me against the wall, kissing my neck while undoing my shirt.

"You're so fucking hot," he tells me in between kisses. "You know this, right?"

I try to stop his hands, but he knocks mine away.

"Stop. I want to do this for you."

"I told you, I'm fine. I've just got a lot on my mind."

"I know something to take your mind off whatever's bothering you." He runs his hands down my chest, over my abs, to my belt.

I try to stop him again. "Really, I'm good."

"I'll be the judge of that," he says as he undoes my fly, diving into my boxer-briefs and taking me in his hand.

Immediately I start to harden, and a smile crosses his face.

"Yeah, you want this. You *need* this."

"Fuck," I say, my head dropping back. I don't want this, but, well, I'm only human.

He rubs me harder, twisting, hitting all the spots I like.

"That's it, babe." He drops to his knees and pulls my pants and underwear down.

"Tell me if I don't do this right," he says before taking me in his mouth.

Automatically my hips push forward, fucking his mouth. I know I shouldn't be doing this, but the look on Cav's face in the hallway.... It was like he was... disgusted with me, that he'd made a mistake, that I wasn't worth the effort. But I am. I gave him *so* many chances to be with me. I waited for him. I gave him everything, and he didn't want it until he couldn't have it. Well, fuck him. The only reason I'm in this mess is because of him.

"Mmm," he moans.

I grab his head, a hand on either side of his face, my hips pistoning, my dick thrusting in and out of his mouth. He gags a couple of times, but I keep going, my release building.

"This what you want?" I grit out. "Me to fuck your mouth?"

"Mmm," he agrees, tears streaming down his face.

"I told you I was fine, but you pushed and you pushed. I didn't want this," I tell him.

He tries to reply, but I don't let him. I let all the anger, frustration, and confusion I've been feeling go, taking it all out on his mouth. I know it's not fair, but he wanted me to let go, to let it out, so I am.

He reaches for his own fly, his pants tented beyond belief.

"This turn you on?" I ask. "Me using you as my plaything?"

He nods once, managing to get his dick out and starting to jerk it.

"That's it," I encourage. "Take everything I give you."

I can feel the tingling at the base of my spine, and I know it won't be long.

"Fuuuuuuuuuuuuuuuuuck," I exclaim, emptying myself down his throat.

He's jerking himself harder, faster, precum weeping from the tip now, when the door opens.

"Seriously?" Cav asks, arms folded over his chest.

I slip from Thomas's mouth as he finally comes.

"Shit, that was good," he says, getting up, not concerned at all with the mess he made. He grabs me by the back of my neck and kisses me.

I stand there, shocked, eyes open, hands at my side, dick flapping in the wind and softer than pudding.

"I don't think I've ever come that hard," Thomas says when he backs away. "Thanks, babe, we should do that more often."

He grabs some paper towel from a nearby shelf and cleans himself up.

The whole time Cav stands there, staring, arms still crossed.

Thomas pulls up his pants and does his fly up before coming over to me.

"As much as I love your body and that huge cock of yours, I don't want everyone to see what's mine," he says, pulling up my own pants and boxers, tucking me away and doing up my pants before buttoning my shirt.

"Er, thanks," I manage.

He gives me a chaste kiss. "You're welcome anytime, babe."

He turns to the door. "Enjoy the show?" he asks Cav.

Cav doesn't say anything, just clenches and unclenches his fists.

"I totally forgot this was one of your spots," Thomas says, "but my guy needed a bit of a stress reliever and it just... popped into my head." He steps out and pats Cav on the chest. "Thanks, man, I owe ya." He then walks away, leaving me alone with his former BFF and subject of my fantasies.

"Um," I say, shuffling my feet. "Sorry. I, ah, didn't know

this was your spot." It makes me sick to my stomach that Thomas brought me here knowing it was Cav's spot. And it makes me sicker still to realize what he just walked in on.

"Work out your stress?" he asks.

I scratch the back of my neck. "Not really. Did you, um, leave that rose in my locker this morning?"

"And if I did?"

"Why?" I ask.

"Does it matter?"

"Of course it does." I take a step toward him. "Fuck, Cav, if this was you telling me you're ready—"

"It obviously doesn't mean shit, considering what just went down here." He turns away, but I grab his arm.

"Wait, just... wait," I plead.

He shakes his head and frees his hand from my grasp. "It's too late. There's no point."

"But there is," I insist.

He gives a wry chuckle. "I suppose I shouldn't be surprised. Things always work out this way for me."

"No, Cav, that's not true. Just give me some time to sort things out and then—"

"Then nothing," he says. "This was a mistake." He gestures between us. "The rose was a mistake, thinking I could be anything other than what I am was nothing but a pipe dream."

I shake my head. "That's not true."

He looks at me, his blue eyes piercing through me. "I hope you guys are happy. You truly deserve each other." With that, he walks away.

The bell rings, and once again I watch Cav get swept away with the crowd.

I want to scream. I want to cry, to rage. I want to rip my hair out, to take back everything to do with Thomas Rose. I want to run through the crowd and find Cav and kiss him and hold him and tell him everything will be all right. But instead, I stand there, lost, not knowing what to do, where to go.

"What the fuck did you do?" Jase rages, emerging from the crowd and shoving me in the chest.

"Nothing. I mean, Thomas and I did something, but it wasn't anything."

"If it wasn't anything, then do you want to explain to me why Cav just rampaged his way through the school, jumped in his car, and tore out of here like a bat out of hell?"

"I didn't know…. I didn't mean…. Thomas and I…. He brought me here. I had nothing to do with it."

"Did you get the rose he put in your locker this morning?" Jase asks.

I nod. "I didn't realize it was from him."

He shakes his head.

"I asked him to wait, that I was going to sort things out, but he wouldn't give me a chance to."

"He was doing what you wanted, Con."

"And I was accepting of that. I just needed some time to end things with Thomas. He wouldn't even give me that."

"He's majorly pissed."

"He doesn't have any right to be. *I* should be the one who's pissed. He didn't give me any time."

"What are you going to do?" he asks.

I blow out a breath. "I don't know. I want to go after him, but I need to talk to Thomas, and I don't even know if he'll talk to me or listen to what I have to say. I don't even know if he wants me anymore." I look at my brother. "Do you know where he's gone?"

He shakes his head. "He didn't say anything to anyone, just stormed off."

"Fuck!" I yell, scaring a few people around us.

My phones buzzes in my pocket, and I dive for it, hoping and praying it's Cav.

Kevin: Oooh, boy, you've made some waves. Cav just texted me, he wants you and him to race this week. Winner takes all. You in?

CHAPTER 41

When I get to the Skids, there's a buzz going around the assembled masses. Seems word got out about Cav's and my race.

It's been two days since he found Thomas and me, and he hasn't been in school since. I've tried calling him, but he's disconnected his "James" number once again.

Jase has been talking to him, I think. He won't tell me or let me talk to him, so I'm not really sure.

I've tried to have a conversation with Thomas several times, but every time he dodges it, spinning the conversation and leaving before I can get to the point. If I didn't know any better, I'd think he knows what's coming and is trying to avoid it. But he can't, can he?

Regardless of what happens with Cav, I know things with Thomas have to end. Really, they never should've started in the first place. I know that now.

As I pull in, I'm directed to the start line, Cav's Chevelle already there, waiting. I park and turn off the car. Kevin greets me.

"Holy shit, boy. This is insane!"

I chuckle.

"I've had people texting me from all parts asking me about this race. People want to see what that R-SPEC can do, especially against Cav's Chevelle."

"Glad I could help," I tell him.

"So you're good with everything, right?"

I nod. "I'm good."

"I have to admit this whole thing took me off guard a little. Cav's not usually so… reckless. He races for cash or the glory. I've never heard of him offering the pink slip before."

"Guess I bring it out in him, then."

He laughs and slaps me on the shoulder. "Whatever you do, keep doing it."

I nod. "Will do."

"We'll get going in a minute. Just have to do a quick check and we're good to go."

"Sounds good."

I look over to Cav, who's shooting daggers at me.

"Can we talk?" I ask as I make my way over to him.

"Nothing to talk about," he says, giving me his back.

I grab his shoulder and spin him around. "There's plenty to talk about."

"No, there's not."

"Please, Cav," I beg. "I want to fix this, make this right."

"Are you still with Thomas?"

"I'm ending it."

"So that's a yes."

"It's an 'I'm leaving him.' I'll leave him for *you*."

He shakes his head. "Don't bother."

"Cav."

"It's fine, Connor. We were a dream anyway, never destined to happen and even more unlikely to last."

"You don't know that."

He gives me a wry smile. "But I do."

"Holy shit, babe," Thomas says, pushing through the crowd, Jase in his wake, and pulling me to him. "This is insane."

"Ah, yeah, it is. Listen, after the race we have to talk, *actually* talk. I've got something really important to say. And what is my brother doing here? You know I don't like him to be alone at these things."

He nuzzles my neck. "He wanted to come, so I brought him. He'll be fine. But we're going to celebrate your win and then we'll talk."

"No, Thomas, we need to talk before anything."

"All right, gentlemen," Kevin says, coming over to us. "One quarter mile drag, winner takes all. Keep it safe, keep it clean, be careful, and good luck."

I nod while Cav gets in his car.

"Good luck, babe," Thomas says, pressing a chaste kiss to my lips.

I walk round and get in my car, securing my seat belt and starting the engine. It purrs beneath me, reacting to the slightest pressure on the gas pedal.

Kevin takes his position between us, checking with both of us once more.

He holds his hands up, the crowd roaring over our engines.

Kevin's hands drop, and I take off, a cloud of burning

rubber behind me. I accelerate quickly, going through the gears; first, second, third.

I look over and see Cav neck and neck with me, his eyes focused on the road except for a quick glance I almost miss.

I go through fourth gear before hitting fifth. The finish line is coming up, and neither of us is giving an inch. I pull ahead, then he does, then we're even.

We hit the line, and I have no idea who won.

Again, I look over at Cav, who this time is definitely looking over at me. I wait for him to ease up, but he doesn't, instead putting his foot down. I follow up, catching him easily.

"What the fuck?" I shout.

He laughs, a smirk pulling at his mouth, his eyes narrowed slightly.

"Cav, stop!" I yell.

I have no idea what he's playing at, but I have to stop him, to talk to him.

He looks back to the road, pulling ahead and in front of me as the road curves. We take it easily, the Skids long forgotten.

I follow him yard for yard, our speeds easily reaching a hundred miles an hour, if not more.

We hit another straight stretch, and I pull out beside him. I hold my hands out as if to say "what the fuck?"

He throws his head back and laughs. I'm so focused on him, on his movement, I don't see the car heading toward us.

I see the headlights in time to swerve, but that's it. My

car tips, then rolls. I don't know how many times I flip. Three? Four? Five? Or what I hit, fence posts, trees, rocks.

I only know that when I eventually come to a stop, I'm upside down, my airbags in my face and along the windows.

My head is pounding, vision blurry. There's pain in my neck, arms, leg, and chest. The smell of gas is heavy in the air. I think I hear people screaming, glass breaking, but it's getting harder to breathe, harder to see, my vision going in and out.

I feel fresh air rush over me, but it doesn't matter; it's not going where it needs to.

I'm gasping, trying to breathe, to focus, but it's all so hard. Blackness is creeping in and taking away all the pain. It's nice there; it doesn't hurt, there's nothing, just peace and quiet and no pain.

"Connor!" I hear someone scream. The voice sounds familiar, but I can't place it.

The blackness creeps in once again, and I'm so tempted to go with it. I'm so tired, I'm just so….

To be Continued

USEFUL LINKS

If you have been affected by any of the issues discussed in this book, please know there are various resources available to you to help get you through your tough time. These are only a very small selection. Please reach out if you, or someone you love needs help. **You are wanted, you are valued, you have a place here.**

Australia.
Lifeline: 13 11 44
QLife: 1800 184 527

Canada.
Canada Suicide Prevention Service: 1 833 456 4566
LGBT Youth Crisis Line: 1800 268 9688

The UK.
Assistline: 0800 689 5652
Mind: 0300 123 3393

The United States.

National Suicide Prevention Lifeline: 1800 273 8255

The Trevor Project: 1 866 488 7386

ABOUT MEGAN

Megan Lowe is a lost journalism graduate who after many painful years searching for a job in that field, decided if she couldn't write news stories, she would start listening to the characters whispering stories to her and decided to write them down.

She writes primarily Mature YA/New Adult/Contemporary Romance stories with a difference.

She is based on the Gold Coast but her heart belongs to New York City.

When she's not writing she's either curled up with a good book, travelling or screaming at the TV willing her sporting teams to pull out the win.

STALKER LINKS!

Website:
www.meganloweauthor.wixsite.com/withadifference

Facebook:
www.facebook.com/MeganLoweAuthor

Amazon:
www.amazon.com/author/meganlowe

Bookbub:
www.bookbub.com/authors/megan-lowe

Goodreads:
www.goodreads.com/meganlowereads

Instagram:
www.instagram.com/meganloweauthor

Twitter:
www.twitter.com/meganloweauthor

meganloweauthor@outlook.com

Sign up to my newsletter:

https://t.co/M31GCdcYtL

OTHER BOOKS BY MEGAN.

Rocking Racers Series

Breaking the Cycle

No Place to Hide

Breaking Away

Breaking Down

All I Want

Breaking Free

Breaking Out

Breaking Ground

Read today here: books2read.com/rl/rocking-racers

Sovereigns of Savannah

Royal Blue

The Good Boy/Bad Boy duet

Good Boy

Bad Boy